POE PARK

POE PARK

by Agnes Martinez

Holiday House / New York

An excerpt from *Annabel Lee* by Edgar Allen Poe appears on p. 41

Library of Congress Cataloging-in-Publication Data
Martinez, Agnes.
Poe Park / by Agnes Martinez—1st ed.
p. cm.
Summary: After graduating from his fifth-grade class in the Bronx,
Enoch looks forward to spending time with his best friend Spence,
but must instead cope with grief, gang violence, and the arrival
from Puerto Rico of his half-brother Miguel.
ISBN 0-8234-1834-0 (hardcover)
[1. Friendship—Fiction. 2. Best friends—Fiction. 3. Death—Fiction.
4. Gangs—Fiction. 5. Brothers—Fiction. 6. Puerto Ricans—Fiction.
7. Bronx (New York, N.Y.)—Fiction.] I. Title.
PZ7.M367125Po 2004
[Fic]—dc22
2004047256

To my parents, Victor and Doris,
and my sisters, Mimi and Vicky,
you are my world.
Without you this book
would not be possible.

Barbara Seuling and
The NYC Manuscript Workshop,
you helped me grow this book.
I am forever grateful.

For all the students who crossed my life
and left their footprints on my heart,
this book is for you.

POE PARK

Chapter 1

Knock. Knock. Who's there? Enoch. Enoch who? Enoch Morales. That's my name. My best buddy, Spencer, calls me Eno. I like the way he says it. It makes me sound cool and special.

Today Spence has his head down on his desk. He is deep into some zzzs while the teacher, Ms. Brea, reads aloud from this book of Greek mythology. I wish I could doze too, but I'm crazy excited. It takes everything I've got to sit still. In one of the stories, this guy steals fire and gives it to the poor people to make their lives better. This makes the God Boss supa angry. He ties the guy to a cliff so the eagles can peck at his guts for eternity. The girls go, "Ohhh, gross!"

Eternity? That's stupid. He'd be dead, what with birds feasting on his insides. Ms. Brea explains that his guts grow back every morning so the birds can do their thing.

I hear behind me, "Yeah, it's payback for crossing the chief."

"No mercy," another voice chimes in.

Together they chant, "No mercy! No mercy!"

I don't have to turn my head to know Adrian and Sam are slapping each other high fives.

Ms. Brea clears her throat and flips the page. She starts another story. I hope it ends better than the last one. Everybody is still buzzing. Everybody except Spencer. He's still in *siesta*.

Nobody wakes him. Even Adrian and Sam don't dare. Ms. Brea glances in Spencer's direction. I notice she gets this look, the kind I've seen on adults where their eyebrows meet in a wrinkle that means worry. Pretty soon, I'm worrying, too. I'm like that: I catch whatever people are feeling. Mami says, "Enoch, you're sensitive." I say, Get out of here with that. I'm not soft and fluffy, although I could stand to lose a pound or two.

Now, my boy Spence, he's street. He's always telling me I oughta get more street, like it's something you can buy at the corner bodega. "Hey, Mister, gimme two pounds of street to go. Cut it nice and juicy thick."

The only thing street about me is my address. *Oye,* between you and me, the real slice is that Mami sweeps the street away from me. She is on me all the time, caring for me, making me all *yon-yon* like a baby. Sometimes it's not so bad. Sometimes it's too embarrassing. What can I say? See, it's only us two. Sometimes I wonder what if, but today I am wondering how I am going to make it through the school day.

Anyhow, Ms. Brea is busy reading about a girl nymph and a god. Even though it sounds like a sappy love story, the action isn't bad. Usually, I enjoy it when people read, getting the pictures in my head like I'm in my own private movie theater: *Cine de Enoch.* Today I have to admit if you asked me what just happened in the story, I'd be in trouble—"Tell me or I'll tie you to the flagpole outside the classroom window so the pigeons can poop on you for eternity"—I'd say, "Tie away—just don't tie knots too tight and let me keep my cap."

You want to know the reason I can't concentrate? Tomorrow is graduation. Then summer vacation begins, and if that wasn't sweet enough, my birthday, the big 1-1, falls on the first day of summer vacation.

I'll be in *fiesta* mode all summer. Go, Enoch. Go, Enoch. Go, Enoch.

Adiós, elementary school.

Adiós, desks where your legs don't fit.

Adiós, cubbies without privacy so your stuff is up for grabs.

Adiós, land of the little kids.

Hel-lo, summer! Just twenty minutes away.

Hey! a spitball misses my ear. I spin around. Sam has switched seats next to the girls. Adrian is tagging his binder. Spencer still has his head down on his desk. His eyes are shut tight, and he has this so slick smile on his lips.

Chapter 2

I graduated! I've got photos to prove it. Mami took pictures of me in my sharp suit. I got to tell you, I looked fine. In one picture, Spence poked his goofy face out from behind my back. Mami says she'll let me keep that one. I know right where it's going—on the wall next to my bed. Mami thinks I shouldn't be tacking things on the wall. She got me a bulletin board a while ago, but it kept falling down and clunking me on the head. I told her that I couldn't sleep because I kept wondering when it would come crashing down on me and then when I finally did get some sleep, I had these terrible dreams that I was trapped under a humongous bulletin board. I couldn't breathe or move.

Mami is used to me, so she just waves her hand. "*Ya!* Enough, Enoch. Okay. Go back to tacking everything on the wall."

Bueno. My wall. On my wall I have pictures of Mami and me, my grandparents in Puerto Rico, my godmother, Miriam, who's a police officer, and her daughter, Carmen, one picture of my dad, and lots of pictures of me with Spence. We've been friends for forever, really since kindergarten. If you asked me how we hooked up, I'd say it just kind of happened. We were line partners and from there it was easy, *suave,* like stuff that's meant to be. Through the years, we've shared our lunches, played together, sometimes battled, got in trouble together, sat next to each other in class (that's if the teacher didn't have it in her mind to separate us), and we've always walked home together. We live a couple of blocks from each other.

Good things should stay as they are. They shouldn't be messed with. Just when you think you have it made, it's like, gotcha. Today would have been *perfecto,* if . . .

See, this is what happened. Mami was taking me out to celebrate, sort of a graduation/pre-birthday feast. We were set to dine at Benny's Ristorante. The owners, Benny and his wife, Nitza, come from the same town, Sabana Grande, Puerto Rico, as Mami. When we walk through the door, they always welcome us like family. They feed us like we're royalty. The food is too *delicioso,* and we get all we can eat—refills of this, doubles of that, special orders, whatever. While you eat, Benny keeps the place humming, checking tables, making sure everything is *cheverre*—okay—and Nitza plays the piano—mostly boleros, Spanish mush music. Mami sings along. I like hearing her sing. Sometimes Mami tells me these funny stories about herself as a little girl on the island. It's always a happy time at Benny's.

So here we are, Mami and I, ready to leave our apartment building to catch a cab for Benny's, when Mami stops, says, "Wait, let me check the mail."

I'm standing next to her, wondering if I should order the beefsteak or the roasted pork. Mami opens the mailbox. There it is. One lonely envelope. Mami reads the return address, then rips it open like it's a check or something. It isn't a check. It's a letter, and Mami is reading it as if it's top-secret instructions, her eyes flicking back and forth.

"What is it, Ma?"

I want to get going. I'm hungry.

"Enoch, *hijo. Es un milagro.*" She holds the letter to her heart.

Now, when Mami starts talking miracles, it's serious stuff. My stomach is stone silent.

"*Hijo,* you are off the waiting list."

Mami sees the question mark on my face.

"Remember? They put you on a waiting list for that new charter school near Fordham University."

How could I forget? A few months ago, Mami found out about this school from a customer at the salon. The lady had all the specifics in her purse, the name and phone number of the school's director. That afternoon Mami called and set up an interview for me on the next day. I didn't want to do it. I figured I would go to the nearby junior high school like everybody else. Mami insisted.

"Enoch, *papito,* I know it's hard to leave your friends, but for some reason this opportunity presented itself. It's a sign. I have been so worried. You don't think I know. Every day there are police cars parked in front of that school. Miriam tells me stories."

"Ma, don't worry—they have metal detectors."

"Metal detectors! That's supposed to make me feel better? Imagine, every morning, children passing through metal detectors. *Qué mundo.* No, Enoch. You are going to interview. Case closed. *Punto!*"

So I interviewed under extreme duress. Mami muttering, "*Oye,* smile. So help me, if you give a bad impression on purpose . . . Smile." I didn't exactly smile, but I was polite and answered all the questions they asked.

As luck would have it, I didn't get in. They didn't have enough seats. I got placed on a waiting list instead. Mami was mad. She said they shouldn't get people's hopes up. I tried not to look too happy.

Case closed. Nothing to worry about, until this afternoon. The letter Mami was clutching said they had opened up enrollment and I was accepted—see you in September. *Ay!*

When Benny and Nitza found out the good news, they hugged and kissed me—congrats. Rats. Tasty food in front of me, and all I could do was pick and nibble here and there. Nitza even played "Happy Birthday" for me on the piano, Mami singing to me.

It would have been *perfecto,* but . . .

What will Spence say when I tell him I'm going to another school? We were supposed to be together.

Chapter 3

Ooo-pa-le! Next day, I spring out of the bed, extra early. Why? It's my big bang b-day and the start of summer fun. I feel like eating a man-size breakfast. I am all in the fridge, looking for the leftover food I didn't finish off at Benny's last night.

"*Buenos días, papito,*" Mami calls as she passes by the kitchen. "*Ay,* look at the time. I have Dona Estelle coming for highlights this morning."

Mami is rushing around like it's just another ordinary day. She's playing the game. It's the same every year. Mami says we are going to celebrate my birthday just the two of us. Then she goes and plans this huge *fiesta* at the beauty parlor. I play along: "Wow, you shouldn't have."

Mami calls from the bathroom, "*Hijo,* meet me at the salon this afternoon—twelve sharp. We'll go to the movies or something."

Uh-hmm.

When she gets ready to leave, I see her searching for her keys. She is always misplacing them. As I help her, looking on the kitchen counter, I figure this is my chance.

"Mami. What if, let's say, I don't accept. What if I say no to that school."

Mami stops and looks at me for a long couple of seconds. Then she flops down on a kitchen chair and I sit next to her.

"Why?"

"I just don't feel that school is for me."

"Who is it for?"

"Somebody else. Not me."

"Enoch, give me a real reason. I'm listening."

"I won't have any friends there, Ma."

"You'll make new friends."

"I don't want new friends. I like the ones I have."

"Enoch. If I could list all the things I didn't want to do but had to do, it would be a *tremenda* list." Mami's hand touches my cheek. "Enoch, baby, happy birthday. I don't know what to say. I just want you to be safe. *Ay!* Is that the time? We'll talk more about this later."

I know what she means. Talk. Talk. She won't change her mind.

"Remember, twelve o'clock sharp." Mami's quick good-bye kiss buzzes my cheek.

Through the window, I see her as she crosses the street. She looks up, waves at me, and smiles. I see that smile a lot. Like I said, it's only Mami and me. That's because my father was killed when he lost control of the truck he was driving during a snowstorm. He died instantly. Mami was pregnant with me at the time, so I never saw him. He never saw me. There's this blank spot in my life when it comes to my father. I don't like to think about him. I usually don't, but today being my birthday, well, I just wonder what it would be like if he was around. Spencer says I'm lucky I didn't know him, 'cause you can't miss what you never had. Maybe he's right.

Thinking of Spence, I bet he'll figure I think I'm too good to go to the regular junior high. Maybe he won't want to be my friend. I have to explain to him that this is all Mami's idea.

My big bang b-day won't be right if I don't settle with Spence. I need to see him.

Spencer lives exactly eight buildings away from me. I could get to his door blindfolded. The downstairs intercom has been broken so many times that now it stays broken. Someone scribbled with a marker next to the buttons, DON'T BOTHER. GO ON UP. So I just go up. Skip the elevator. That's not working either. No sooner do I hit the stairs when I see Spencer. At first he doesn't notice me. He's charging down the steps two and three at a time.

As he passes me, I go, "Hey!"

Spencer does a double take like I startled him. Then he smiles. "Hey, Eno!"

"Where you going?" I laugh, thinking that he's probably heading over to me. No response. My buddy opens his mouth as if to tell me, but nothing comes out. So I ask again.

"Where you going?"

Then I hear a voice coming from the flight of stairs below us.

"Spence! What's keeping you? Let's go!"

It's Dougie, Spencer's teenage cousin.

"Coming!" Spencer yells back. He turns to me and smiles. "Eno, I'm bringing a surprise to your party. See you later. Wait." He runs up and punches my shoulder so quick I don't have time to react.

Dougie's voice booms off the walls.

"Spencer!"

"Birthday punch number one!" my buddy calls out as he bounds down the stairs.

Normally I'd chase after Spencer and tag along. We're always in each other's business, but today, for whatever reason, he was with Dougie. I keep distance between Dougie and me. You would too if you heard the stories Spencer tells about his older cousin. That Dougie, he wasn't so bad before. Then about a year ago, he joined a street crew, Firearms, and he's been wild ever since. Word is he's been picked up a couple times by the police.

I walk around, hands in my pockets, checking out the beautiful, sun-in-your-face day as I make my way up the Concourse to Mami's beauty parlor, Lourdes' Salon. All the *viejas* in the neighborhood go there. These old ladies are my mom's *comadres,* gossip pals, and they're a real pain. They tell my mother whenever they see me doing something I shouldn't. "Lourdes, I saw your boy, Enoch, roller-skating in the middle of traffic. *Madre mía,* he came this close to getting run over."

Then there go the skates.

Today three *viejas*—Dona Ida, Dona Estella, and Dona Sylvia—are helping Mami decorate the place with balloons and streamers. This kid Julio, who just started working regular at the salon as a stylist, is tacking up a gold foil *Feliz Cumpleaños* banner over the mirror.

Everyone is so busy, they don't notice me. Can you believe it? Finally I clear my throat—hmmfff. You know, like people do on TV when they want somebody to pay attention.

You think everyone would be glad to see the birthday boy?

"*Ay, niño!*" Mami jumps back when she sees me. "Didn't I specifically tell you twelve o'clock sharp? Not eleven o'clock. Twelve o'clock. I wanted you to see everything ready and be surprised."

Dona Estella looks at me funny. She whispers to Mami. "*Bendito,* Lourdes, maybe he has a hearing problem."

Dona Ida clicks her tongue. "The boy's hearing is fine. Children nowadays just don't appreciate anything."

"Hmm. Hmm. I have a niece like that. *Oye.* I could tell you stories." Dona Sylvia presses her lips tight.

Julio suggests a do-over.

So I walk out of the salon and come back in again like I don't know anything.

This time they all shout in unison, "Happy birthday, Enoch!"

It's so silly. I watch my face in the mirror as I act surprised. What a performance! I ought to be an actor.

Later, guests arrive. Quiet Willy, the son of the man who owns the dry cleaners next to us, comes with his mom. They sit silently on the chairs by the open door. At super velocity, Kareem, Leon, and Baby Omarr, Spencer's little brothers, come racing in. Mrs. Bandy, Spencer's grandma, huffing and puffing, is right on their heels. "Mind your manners," I hear her say as Kareem and Leon make a grab for the chips. I ask her where Spencer is. "He's coming, sugar," she says as she catches Baby Omarr before he goes under a table. Carmen, my godsister, steps in with her mom, my *madrina*, Miriam. They are carrying a cake for you-know-who. Then Sam, Dona Estella's grandson, waltzes in with his friend Adrian. If it was up to me, I wouldn't invite these two gangsta wannabes to my party, but Mami says Dona Estella is having a hard time with Sam at home. No kidding. Mami says he could use some positive influences. What does it matter if he's always hanging with Adrian? Anyway, I'm not going to let it spoil my day.

Pretty soon the salon is packed. It's jamming. The Latin beat fills the salon courtesy of Julio's boom box. When people get tired of dancing, they load up their plate with roasted pork, fried plantains, and yellow rice with pigeon peas. *Delicioso!* The birthday cake Miriam and Carmen brought me is looking so scrumptious. It's my favorite, chocolate with custard filling.

The rhythm of the conga drums makes my shoulders groove. Mami takes my hand and we dance. She taught me how when I was a baby— salsa, merengue, whatever. I just add my own style. Maybe I ought to be a dancer.

Miriam wants to turn down the music so I can blow out the birthday candles. I start to say wait. Someone isn't here. Then I see Spencer coming through the door holding a shoe box. Like always, he has this huge grin on his face.

Mami lights the candles. All the people stop dancing. The little kids even stop chasing one another. I close my eyes and pretend I'm wishing up a whole list of things, then I blow. Truth is, I wished for one thing: that I won't have to go to that stupid charter school.

Miriam and Mami can't lay down the plates of cake fast enough to please this crowd. I take my piece and head to one of the swivel seats. Spencer is sitting with his grandma. Quiet Willy is sitting in the seat next to me. We nod at each other. Our mouths are full of cake, which is just as well. Quiet Willy is not a talker. Everyone thinks he's a weirdo kid. I feel sorry for him. He gets the best grades in school, but he's always alone. Sam has Adrian, and I have Spencer. Even Carmen, who can get along with anybody, steers clear of Quiet Willy.

Just as I polish off the crumbs on my plate, Spencer joins me. Under one arm he holds the shoe box, and in the other a plate of cake. Somehow he managed to get a second helping.

Spencer hands me the box.

"Surprise!"

I feel something slithering around inside the box. I ask Spencer if it's a snake. He just opens his eyes wide and pretends like he doesn't know what I'm talking about. Boy, I hate snakes. Spencer thinks they are so cool. He once saw a man walking down the Concourse with a snake wrapped around his neck, and he actually asked the man if he could pet it. Pet it! If it was up to Spencer, he'd have his own snake, but his grandma won't let that happen. So I wonder if he's giving one, the next best thing to having one. He could visit it every day. Imagine that.

"Open the box already," Spencer says, lifting the lid. It's not a snake. It's an iguana. Not a bad-looking iguana, either. It's about ten inches long, bright green. Spencer points out its bluish markings, striped tail, and long dorsal spines. He tells me that it's trained to ride on people's shoulders. Nice, but it looks kind of expensive. I'm going to ask him how much it costs when I hear a squeaky voice behind me. It's Carmen. Like I said, she's my godmother's daughter. Carmen's a year younger than me. I use to think she was okay, but lately she's been acting stranger than Quiet Willy. You'll catch her staring at you. You ask her, "What's up?" She doesn't say a word. Just smiles. Or she'll stand up so close to you. It gives me the creeps. Mami says Carmen has a crush on me. That is scary.

"Can I hold it? Please. Please." Carmen doesn't wait for the lizard to blink. She reaches out, takes it in her arms, and rocks it. If the iguana could talk, it would have said, "Save me! Save me!" Carmen asks if it is a boy or girl.

"A boy," Spencer mumbles; his mouth is full of cake. I watch the little iguana traitor nuzzle in the crook of Carmen's arm.

Then Carmen looks at me real serious, like she's mad. When was I going to open her present? She pointed to a small package on the gift table.

Mami is always telling me to be polite. Say thank-you like you really mean it.

Carmen went on, all about how she designed the wrapping paper from a recycled brown bag and decorated it with stamps and glitter. Lucky she told me that, 'cause I usually rip and tear to get to the gift. Now I carefully peel the wrapping off a box of—can you believe this?—aftershave. Spencer smirks.

Thank-you like you really mean it. Yeah, right.

"Happy Birthday." Carmen's face is suddenly next to mine, and before I know it, she's kissing my cheek.

A blinding light hits me in the eyes. Mom snapped the picture.

"*Qué lindo.* How cute!"

I'd been set up. Spencer says my face was mad red.

Chapter 4

My *fiesta* came and went, and I didn't talk to Spencer about September. What with one thing and another, it didn't come up. Besides, at the end of June, September seems so far away. Lots of things can happen in two months.

You know, I've decided to call my iguana Isadore—nickname Izzy. I'm still not comfortable holding him yet. Anyway, it's good for a joke.

"Izzy Iguana?"

"Of course he is, stupid."

Sometimes I kill myself.

After Mami went to work, I called Spencer. Dougie answered on the first ring.

"Who's this?"

"Enoch. Can I talk to Spencer?"

"Boy. He's sleeping. What are you doing calling people at this hour? You ought to know better than that."

I glanced at the kitchen clock. It was ten to eight. "Sorry," I muttered.

"It's all right. Guess you're excited. After all, yesterday was your birthday. How old are you now? Ten?"

"Eleven," I corrected him.

Dougie's deep laughter filled my ear. "Whoa, you're grown! You're a little man. Happy birthday. Listen, call back in a couple hours and maybe Spencer can come out to play with you. Now I got to go bye-bye 'cause I am waiting on a call."

He hung up.

Talking with Dougie left me confused and angry. I'm just glad I don't have to live with him. Spence says he's not so bad, that he teaches him cool stuff.

Call back in a couple of hours. I set the alarm on my new wristwatch for 10 A.M. A birthday present, one of many. Mami put a stack of thank-you cards on my dresser. I'll have to write them with her nearby. She doesn't exactly trust me. I'll want to say something meaningful, like, "Carmen, the aftershave will come in handy for killing flies." Mami will want me to say, "Thank you for the lovely aftershave. Whenever I put it on, I'll think of you." *Ay!*

I turned on the TV, but it was beat. I've seen these episodes a million times before.

It was only nine o'clock. I wanted so bad to call Spencer. What if Dougie answered the phone again? Nah. I decided to wait.

So I spent the rest of the morning safeguarding the apartment for Isadore. I checked the screens on the windows. I plugged up the hole in the floor near the radiator with an old sock. I used an old sweat suit for the bottom of the refrigerator and the stove.

Isadore keeps getting out of the punch bowl Mom gave me to keep him in. What I really ought to do is buy him a glass tank with a lid, but I'm not going to waste my allowance on it. I have plans for that money, plans that spell S-U-M-M-E-R F-U-N, Spencer, wake up!

*   *   *

Something weird is going on. You know, after I waited until ten to call Spencer, his grandmother said he had left.

I guess it's happening already. Spencer is forgetting his homeboy, Enoch. What will happen in September when we're in different schools? Well, fine—be like that, buddy.

What am I waiting for? Summer has started. Here I have this bike propped against my wall. It's looking so squeaky brand-new, ready for some use. I got the bike after the *fiesta*. While I was helping clean up, Mami wheeled something shiny in front of me. The bike came with a big silver bow and a warning: "Enoch! *Muchacho!* If I hear you're riding it in the Concourse traffic, you lose it!"

Time's a-wasting.

I pedal fast, past the people on the wooden benches, around the white-and-green rotunda where they're setting up speakers for some band to play, and then I brake in front of the dead writer's house—Poe Cottage.

I've been going to Poe Park since I was a little kid. Mom doesn't like me hanging around there anymore. A couple of weeks ago, a woman in our building got mugged as she walked through the park on her way home from work. They must have been following her, 'cause they got her pay envelope for the week.

I told Mom I know how to take care of myself. I promised I wouldn't go to Poe Park after 7 P.M.

I thought that was a cool compromise, but Mami's response was "*Muchacho,* someday you are going to kill me." Mami can spread the guilt like butter.

Poe Park is on 196th Street and the Grand Concourse in the Bronx. It faces P.S. 246, my old school. Poe Park is not your average park. For one thing, it doesn't have a handball court or playground. For that, you have to go a block or two to St. James Park. What Poe Park has is benches, benches, benches. It's a sit-down, hang-out type of place. In the summer, oooh-eee, it is sizzling *caliente* with activity.

Like at one point—I see a guy slipping a small envelope into the shirt pocket of another guy doing curls with hand weights. Drugs? I don't look too hard. Next to them a group of teenage girls try out the latest dance steps. They look good and they know it. The *viejos,* the old men, play dominoes while a man and a woman dressed in their church clothes scream into a microphone about what it's going to be like when the world ends. In a corner, not to be left out, a homeless bum recites poetry to the pigeons. Spencer and I like to goof on the people in Poe Park. Wait a sec, you know what I'm doing? I'm wasting the day. I've got to plan the summer before it mega-rockets by.

Things to Do with No *Dinero*	Things to Do with *Dinero* $$$$$$$
1. Swim at the Y	1. Buy ices, pizzas, and burgers
2. Ride my bike	2. Go to the movies
3. Roller-skate	3. Rent video games
4. Go to the library	4. Buy firecrackers
5. Play handball	5. Go to Yankees games
6. Play basketball	

It's really hot, and I can't think of anything else to add to my list. I figure I'd better head home. Before I go, I buy a *coquito,* a coconut ice, from a little white cart outside the park. I like coconut ice so much, sometimes I feel like sucking it up and swallowing the paper cup it comes in.

I see Spencer. He's across the Concourse, and he's waving for me to join him. It's about time, Spence, my boy.

I had a chance to tell my buddy about September, but again I let it fly. All the kids wanted a ride on my bike.

"Come on, Enoch—please, please, please."

I only let Spence. I felt him behind me as I pedaled hard. His hands gripped my shoulders.

"Can't you go faster, E-knucklehead?"

I purposely went over a bump.

"Only kidding, Eno." Spencer laughed. If there's one thing about my buddy that drives me crazy, it's that he is always happy. I've never seen him sad. Angry, yeah. Spitting, cussing angry, but sad, nah. Mrs. Bandy, his grandma, calls Spencer her Sunshine Boy. He always looks at her kind of weird when she says that, but it's true. His laugh is like a wave. You have to laugh, too. I always do. That's why I spent most fifth-grade afternoons in detention.

As I rode my bike with Spencer that afternoon, I forgot about September.

Later that night, I can't sleep. It's so hot. I put my face up close to the window screen, hoping to catch a breeze. I hear a bunch of loud bangs outside. In this neighborhood, it's either fireworks or gunshots, and that sounded like gunshots. Maybe not. I move away from the window just in case.

Isadore is resting peacefully in his punch bowl. Who'd have known he'd turn out to be such a troublemaker. Earlier tonight he got lost. I spent an hour looking for him. Someone pulled the sock out of the hole near the radiator and the sweat suit was in the hamper. I told Mami that if Isadore was dead, it was all her fault. She told me she was too tired to argue and she needed a cup of chamomile tea. I heard her rummaging through the kitchen cupboard. Then I heard a cup crash to the floor, followed by Mami screaming like I'd never heard her scream before.

"*Ay! Ayyy! Maldita sea.*"

I ran to the kitchen. There was Isadore hanging on to Mami's back.

"*Quitamelo,* Enoch! Take it off! He jumped on me from the refrigerator. *Quitamelo!* Take it off!" Mami hopped from foot to foot as I pulled Isadore off her shirt.

Then I did something really stupid. I started to laugh, and the timing was awful. Maybe later, like twenty years from now, she would have found the situation funny, but tonight she was not to be messed with.

"*Mira, muchacho!*"

Whenever my mom starts a sentence with "*Mira, muchacho,*" "Look, boy," I know I am in trouble.

Well, I did like "your wish is my command" and scrammed.

The loud bangs are starting up again. *Pop-pop-pa-boom.* Only this time closer. Maybe on the roof. I hope nobody I know is hurt. Mami is in her bedroom. She's not mad anymore. Before I went to bed, I told her good night and that I was sorry. She grinned and took my face in her two hands and kissed my cheek. "Laugh at your own mother." She's a good mom. I wish she didn't have to work so hard.

The people downstairs are arguing. I can't make out what they're saying, but boy, they sound furious. I wonder if Spencer is having trouble sleeping, too. He shares a bed with his brothers Kareem and Leon. Those two little guys are non-stop on-the-go tykes. They're never still. Spencer says they make a fuss when it's time to sleep. Mrs. Bandy has to show them the belt just so they'll settle down.

Spencer is crazy about his brothers. We have a lot of fun with them. Kareem and Leon believe everything you say. Whenever they want to follow us around, we tell them they can't come because it's too dangerous. Spencer and I are top-secret-agent superheroes and we're always on a case. We've saved the world a bunch of times. If Kareem and Leon behave, we'll train them. Train them, we do. We have wild training sessions. Mrs. Bandy lets us. We set up obstacle courses in the living room. Even Baby Omarr joins in. He is the biggest, strongest baby I have ever met. He has got a grip that you wouldn't believe. It is so hilarious watching Spencer arm-wrestle with him.

He lets Baby Omarr win, but one day—watch out.

Everything is fun, except when Dougie walks through.

Sometimes when Spencer sleeps over and it's really late and we can't fall asleep, Spencer talks about Dougie. He talks about his mom, who's living in the streets, and his dad, who's doing time. I lie quietly listening to my buddy tell me things like when his grandma shut the door on his mother when she showed up drugged out and wanted her kids. Or when they took his dad away.

Spence tells me things he wouldn't tell anybody else and vice versa. It's important to have a friend you can talk to.

Maybe Spencer can sleep over Fourth of July weekend. I'll ask Mom.

Chapter 5

The next day, at Gino's Pizzeria, I am melting like the mozzarella. It's really hot. The newspapers are predicting that it's going to get hotter, something like 100 plus. Spencer has the front of his shirt hiked over his head.

A little while ago Spencer and I were chilling in Poe Park, when we had what I guess you can call a confrontation. It all started when I suggested we go bag some groceries at the twenty-four-hour food mart—that way we could pick up some change and some AC.

Spencer said he didn't need to bag groceries ever again. Then he pulled out a twenty-dollar bill and made like he was shining his sneaker with it. Hey, what's going on? I wanted to know.

"You're just a baby. I'll tell you when you get older," Spencer said.

That did it. Without warning, I jumped on Spencer and pinned his arms back. Spence thought this was hysterical. After all, he's got about ten pounds and three and one-quarter inches in height on me, but I'm two months and nine days older. I kind of waited for Spence to flatten me, but he didn't.

"Eno, easy. Easy. I found the money on the Concourse. Okay?"

"Okay," I said. It felt good to make a stand and not get creamed.

Life sure is *loco,* arguing one minute, sharing pizza the next.

This would have been a great time to tell Spence about September.

Through the pizza shop window, I see a fire hydrant going full blast. Even with the sprinkler the fire department had put on last week, gushes of water spouted high. A bunch of kids are having a ball running through it. Spencer is standing up, looking at them, too.

"Hey, Eno, last one in still pees his bed," he calls as he darts out. I'm right behind him.

If you ask me what happened next, I can only tell it standing outside of it, as if it were a trailer for a bad movie. It keeps playing over and over.

Coming soon to a theater near you: Enoch and Spencer throw off their shirts and jump into the spray of water, squeezing between all the other kids at the hydrant. The water feels crazy good. Spencer spins in circles, getting wet all over, while Enoch dodges around him. Just as he gets ready to leap on Spencer, Enoch hears, *Pa-pa-pa-pop.* Then Spencer's knees give away and he crumples into a heap. "What'sa matter, buddy?" Enoch squats next to Spencer and sees blood dripping out of his friend's chest like he has sprung a leak.

Everyone is screaming. Parents rush to get their kids. Enoch feels himself being lifted away from Spencer. All he can think of is: No. No. Don't let Spencer's blood flow faded red down the sewer. He's going to need it. Please. No. End of preview. Replay.

This the worst day of Enoch's life. My life.

Chapter 6

After the ambulance took Spencer, I ran as fast as I could to his apartment. I banged and kicked on his door. No one was home.

"What's the problem!" A neighbor swung open her door and came out into the hall. She had her arms across the front of her housecoat. "You kids, I've had it with you. Always making noise like no one else matters."

"Do you know where Mrs. Bandy is?"

"Well, you can pound your fists on the door like a little maniac and she's not going to answer you, 'cause she's downstairs doing laundry."

No sooner had she said that than I bounded down the steps to the basement. The laundry room was empty except for a man taking clothes out of the dryer.

"I'm looking for Mrs. Bandy."

"If you mean the lady that was here, the cops came and got her. Seems that something happened to one of the kids she takes care of. These are her clothes. I told her I'd take care of them for her. I hardly know the lady. I see her around some with all those kids. Reminds me of my old lady, forever trudging with little ones. So I did her the favor, though I don't have the time. I have a list of things to do that hangs out the door. After this—"

Mami always tells me that interrupting people when they are talking is rude, but this guy didn't show any signs of stopping, so I jumped in: "Do you know where they went?"

"Who?"

"Mrs. Bandy and the police!" I screamed.

"Can't say I do. Only know that she was real upset. That's why I—"

I left the guy with the words in his mouth. I had to get to Spencer and make sure he was all right.

I sprinted to Mami's salon. Julio just about had a heart attack when he saw me. *"Ay, Dios mío!*

You're okay?" Julio pinched my arms as if he was trying to make sure I was real. Then he started in with these wild dramatic gestures. "Where have you been? Your mother is out of her mind. Out of her mind. *Loca.* She went to the police precinct! Somebody said you got shot or something. *Imaginate.*"

"It wasn't me. It was my buddy." I turned to leave.

Julio hopped in front of me. "Where are you going?"

"I have to find out where they took Spencer."

"No, *señor*! You wait until your mother comes." Julio blocked the door.

You know, Julio is as skinny as they come. I was getting ready to bum rush the door when the telephone rang and rang. I could hear Mami's clear voice on the answering machine.

"Julio. Julio. Did Enoch show up? I feel terrible. His friend Spencer didn't make it to the hospital."

I leaped over the counter and grabbed the phone.

"Ma. What happened?"

"Enoch? Are you all right?"

"You were saying about Spencer."

Mami was silent.

"Oh, baby. I know you were such good friends. I'm so sorry." Mami's voice cracked. When I heard Mami say the *d* word, I threw the phone down and ran out of the shop.

I sat in Poe Park trying to figure out how this day had happened. It didn't make sense. Maybe Mami had the wrong information. People are always slipping you wrong info. Like she thought I was the one who was in trouble when it was Spencer. Maybe right now Spencer's smiling, telling his grandma that everything is fine. He's always playing jokes on people.

A mess of a bum with matty long hair circled around the bench and sat next to me. I had seen this guy lots of times hanging around Poe Park.

"Good afternoon," he said to no one in particular as he pulled out a small bottle of liquor from his knapsack. I moved down to the end of the bench, giving him my meanest *monstruo* stare. He looked my way, raised his bottle as if in a toast, and then walked himself to the opposite end of the bench, away from me. *Bueno.*

Then the bum started talking to himself, loud, so the whole park could hear:

> *"It was many and many a year ago,*
> *In a kingdom by the sea,*
> *That a maiden there . . . "*

Oh, who cares? Shut up.

> *". . . lived whom you may know*
> *By the name of Annabel Lee."*

Ay, Spence. My buddy. I should have stayed with you. I should have gotten in the ambulance. Though we don't look alike, I could have said we were *hermanos,* brothers. Adopted brothers. Why didn't I do that?

> *"And this maiden she lived with no other thought*
> *Than to love and be loved by me."*

*   *   *

I guess I'd been sitting there for a while when a police car cruised by and honked its horn.

"Enoch." It was Miriam.

I knew Mami had sent her to look for me. I didn't want to stay in the park. I didn't want to go home.

Miriam waited a minute. Seeing I wasn't coming, she got out of the car. She looked at me, then at the bum, who was now hunched over, asleep.

"Hey, kiddo. I don't blame you for being upset. I know about Spencer."

"Mami says he didn't make it," I whispered, hoping she'd tell me something different.

"Your mom's right. The bullet hit a major artery. He died on the way to the hospital. I'm sorry." Miriam, the cop, sat down. "We are still trying to figure out what happened. Enoch, I know it's rough, but I need to ask you a couple of questions. It's my job. Forgive me, *papi*. I wish I didn't have to do this." Miriam hesitated before pulling out her notebook. Her eyes were as wet as mine. She started her questions with the obvious one. Did I see who might have done this? No. "Take your time. Think carefully, Enoch." All I could see was Spencer laid out on the wet street. The paramedics were all over him. Everything else faded around that. Blank spots. As hard as I tried, I couldn't fill them in.

"I don't remember."

"Was there anything suspicious before the shooting?"

"I don't remember."

"After?"

"I don't remember."

"Anything unusual with Spencer?"

"Nothing. Well . . ."

"What?"

I told Miriam about the twenty dollars Spencer had and how we fought and made up. After all, Spencer had said he found the money on the Concourse. Miriam started making a big deal about this, like Spencer had done something wrong. I flipped.

"Stop! Spencer's good. If he said he got the money on the Concourse, I believe him. You should, too."

Miriam closed her notebook. "Maybe later it will be easier to talk about this. Let's get out of here."

Chapter 7

Next day, I wake up, forgetting. You know how it is. It's one-two-three. You open your eyes. You sit up. You even get on your feet. Then it's the knockout punch. The bad news from the day before. You're left stunned.

I look at the photos of Spencer on my wall and moan. Mami has been up for some time. I can tell by the way she's cooking, as she mashes garlic and mixes it with *sofrito*. I stand beside her.

"Enoch. *Hijo*. How are you? Sit down. I'll warm up your breakfast." I notice her eyes are puffy. I know mine must be worse.

Suddenly I can't speak. It's like if I do, I'll lose it. I'm not afraid to cry in front of my mother. Last night I cried more than I've cried all my life. It's just that I never had much to cry about before, so turning off the waterworks had never been a problem. Until yesterday.

Mami tells me that she got the idea to cook these meals for Spencer's family because when my dad died, their friends sent her baskets of fruit and casseroles. Poor Mrs. Bandy is in no condition to cook for herself or her grandchildren. Mami puts a plate of scrambled eggs and toast in front of me. I take a forkful of eggs. I hold it to my mouth. I can't eat. It even hurts to swallow. I know Mami is watching me. She tells me that Spencer's wake will be held tomorrow at the funeral home next to Poe Park. Then they are taking him to North Carolina for the burial. The day after tomorrow is the Fourth of July.

Later I take a long shower. Hot water pelting me. I'm soaping up my hair, when I remember my big problem from a couple days ago. Spencer and I going to different schools in September. Erase that. Soap in your eyes. It doesn't matter anymore. Coming from the bathroom, I purposefully avoid looking at the wall near my bed. Then I notice Mami has taken down all of Spencer's photographs. They're in a large manila envelope on my dresser. I'm glad she did it, sad she did it.

Late afternoon, Mami is dropping off the food at Mrs. Bandy's. Did I want to come? I shake my head. No way. Seeing that apartment, knowing Spencer is gone. No. No. No. I grab the television remote. A game show. Everybody is so stupid-happy on game shows. Jumping-up-and-down happy. Izzy climbs up on my chest. Izzy the iguana. I had forgotten about him completely. I check his food dish. It's almost empty. I'll run and fill it. Izzy.

I don't get wakes. Paying your respects to somebody you care about who is laid out in their best clothes and looking all dead. It's useless. I tell that to Mami.

"It's a way to say good-bye," Mami tells me as we walk down the street to meet Miriam and Carmen. I hope Miriam isn't going to start up with a lot of questions.

"Enoch." Carmen waves. She was all smiles until she saw me. "I'm sorry about Spencer. He sometimes would tease me, but he was very nice to animals."

Spencer did like teasing Carmen. She's the kind of person that believes anything you tell her. Add to that, within seconds of finding out she's been fooled, Carmen'll put her hands on her hips and tell you off. The girl can sure get angry, but just as quick, she'll forget the whole thing. No grudges.

"You look so so sad." Carmen walks up next to me. "Maybe sometime we could go to the movies or something. Or you could come over and we'll play games on my computer. Like we used to."

"Carmen, let's go buy some flowers." Mami motions toward the corner florist that's a block away from the funeral home.

I know it's a ploy. Miriam wants to speak to me. Here it comes: "Enoch, I talked it over with your mother. You should know. We have some kids in custody. They're not from the area. They were running by the hydrant, one of them was playing with a gun. He tripped. The gun went off and killed your friend."

It made sense. It fit the picture of our street. I'd heard Miriam talking with Mami about these things. I know what will happen. What always happens. The killer will be out toting a gun same time next year. Maybe the next time it will be you lying in a puddle of blood. I feel sick. I lean into the nearest trash can and throw up the breakfast Mami made me eat this morning.

Wake over. Down. Done with. Never ever want to do it again. I figured the only way to make it through this was to move fast. Not stop to think. *Imposible* for Enoch Morales. So I walked into the funeral home quickly. In a small room, there was an open casket. There were rows of red velvet chairs. Mrs. Bandy was seated up front, Baby Omarr asleep in his stroller. Next to her, Kareem and Leon sat silently in their little matching suits.

I was supposed to give Spencer's grandmother my condolences. To say I was sorry about what happened to Spencer. The words flew out of my brain when Mrs. Bandy opened her mouth.

"They told me a boy came looking for me after it happened. It was you, wasn't it?" She smiled, tears flowing down her cheeks. "I am so glad that in his short life, he had a friend like you."

What do you say to that? *Sorry* doesn't cut it.

Mrs. Bandy took my shoulder and led me to the casket. "Doesn't the boy look nice?"

I nodded.

"I'll leave you be."

What? I started thinking. Spencer looked like a sleeping *angelito*. Like he could do no wrong. Yeah, he doesn't break a dish. He breaks the whole set of dishes. Like he'd open his eyes any minute and say, "Fooled ya."

I realized this was the first dead person I'd ever seen.

I made up my mind. Right then. Right there. This thing in front of me wasn't Spencer. Like the reptiles he loved so much, my buddy had just shed his skin. That was it. I had nothing. *Nada* to say to dead skin.

I wanted to leave, but Mami said we had to pay respects, which meant staying around and praying.

I slumped in a chair. Carmen sat next to me. "Did you touch him?" she asked in a low whisper.

"Why would I want to do that?"

"Sometimes people do that."

"I didn't."

"I wonder what he feels like."

"He doesn't feel like anything."

Carmen's eyes opened wide. "You think your hand might go right through him like he was a ghost?"

"It might."

"Don't tell me that." Carmen sat back. I had given her a lot to think about. Hey, this one is for you, Spence.

Suddenly there was a commotion. A large group of teens barged into the room. Gang members. They didn't wear colors or have any distinguishing marks, but it's there like the nose on your face. Dougie headed the group that filed past the casket. Mami and Miriam looked extremely serious and tense. Mrs. Bandy had her head down. She was praying either for Spencer, or for Dougie to leave.

With one hand, Dougie touched Spencer's heart, and with the other, he touched his own. Dougie's hand didn't go through Spencer. I think Dougie was crying. As I watched Dougie and his crew go, I thought any one of them could easily kill or be killed. Funny, how Dougie didn't turn or say a word to Mrs. Bandy or his little cousins. He just left.

There are a lot of things in life that I don't understand.

Chapter 8

ndependence Day. This year it arrived louder
than ever. Every couple of minutes the fire-
crackers sizzle, hiss, and boom like small bombs
or they *pa-de-pa-pop* like, you know what. Fire-
crackers? Gunshots? Big deal. I stick headphones
over my ears. I'm going to stay in bed all day and
listen to music. Isadore is on the bedpost, keeping
me company. He's the only company I want. I tell
that much to Mami when she comes by asking if
I want to join Carmen and Miriam. They're going
to Orchard Beach. Are you kidding? Change the
scenery, but you can't change what is. So leave me
alone, thank you. What Mami doesn't know is

that I've decided never, ever to step out of this apartment.

The days clump together. If someone was looking at me with a magic crystal ball, well, they'd find me either sleeping, watching TV, listening to music, or just lying around. As for eating, I'll nibble just enough for Mami not to have a fit. It could be my favorite dessert and I won't want it.

Every now and then Mami comes to me and says, "Enoch, *papito,* let's talk." I turn away. It makes me feel worse. I don't want to take things out on her—that's not right.

"I know you feel bad," Mami says, but she doesn't let up.

She keeps sending people to watch me while she's working. Today it was one of the *viejas,* Dona Felicia. I see her from the corner of my eye as I watch *Jeopardy!* She is praying *el rosario.* Oh, brother.

Another day Julio checks in on me. He fixes me crunchy tuna sandwiches. What makes them crunchy is the pickles and potato chips mixed in the tuna salad. It wasn't half bad. While we watch the Spanish soaps, the *novelas,* Julio talks nonstop about his boyfriend.

That same evening Miriam and Carmen drop by. I sit on the sofa because it's too rude to go to my bedroom and slam the door. You would have expected Carmen to be following me around, but instead she sat on the chair across from the sofa, looking as miserable as me. For a change she kept her lips shut tight.

"She's upset. She got braces put in yesterday. To make matters worse, you know, her father didn't even call her for the Fourth," I overhear Miriam tell Mami as I go to get a glass of water.

"Now, what can you expect? He has a new family. It's not the same." Mami shakes her head.

"Kids. How are you, Enoch?" Miriam kisses my cheek. "You look skinny."

"He's not eating," Mami announced to the world as she handed Miriam a cup of *café con leche.* The aroma fills the kitchen.

"Enoch, *hijo,* remember your manners. Did you ask Carmen what she wants to drink?"

A glass of orange soda. I think that's what Carmen mumbled. Just before I go into the kitchen, I pause, hearing Mami's hushed tone: "I am so worried about him. Ever since this terrible thing happened to his friend, he hasn't been the same."

"Give him time."

"*Dios mío,* Miriam, sometimes I think . . . it could have been my child."

"Lourdes, don't."

When Miriam and Carmen go, I go—straight to my bedroom. I grab the remote control and sprawl myself out on my bed. My little thirteen-inch television has been putting in some serious hours. It is on night-shift duty now.

"*Oye, m'ijo,* the TV is going to blow up." Mami is in the living room talking out loud to the air and hoping that I'm listening. "What you ought to do is come help me out in the salon."

Nope.

I do some mind-boggling channel hopping— news, weather, talk shows, sitcom reruns, stupid movies, info-commercials, anything. Sound off. Sound on. All day. All night. I'm afraid to go to sleep. Whenever I do, I have weird dreams. Last night I dreamed I was playing handball with

Spencer. This homeless guy covered in a blanket from head to toe places empty cans upright in a circle all around us. Spencer and I keep playing, until I knock over a can, then all the cans fall like dominoes. I turn around. Spencer isn't there anymore. I wake up calling his name, white noise on the TV screen.

Tonight I sleep. No dreams I can remember.

Like usual, first thing I do when I get up is I look around for Izzy. He hangs out all over the room, and finding him is like a game. He never hides where I can't find him. Today, though, I can't see him anywhere. I really got to get him a tank.

"Izzy? Where are you?" I'm getting nervous. Finally, I spot him on the floor next to the curtain. Right away, I think he's dead, but I notice he is breathing heavy. His mouth is swollen and yellow stuff is coming out. I run to tell Mami. She makes an appointment to take Isadore to the vet in the afternoon. Only she says I have to come too since I'm his owner. This means I have to go outside.

The minute we leave the apartment, I feel a thumping in my chest like my heart is a jackhammer. Mami asks me if I am all right. Cool. I don't tell her that everywhere I look, there seem to be bad things just waiting to happen. I watch people's faces, thinking, Which ones are packing weapons? I wasn't going to be stupid anymore, trusting all these faces. I walk close to Mami. We catch the bus to the vet's office. A man offers Mami a seat. I stand, holding the sneaker box with Isadore inside with one hand and the pole with the other. I count the street signs that go by. Right before our stop, a couple of kids hop on the bus without paying. They've got this rowdy loud laughter that takes over. I don't know these kids, but I know the type. Show-offs looking for trouble. My school was full of them. One of the kids looks my way, as if to say, "Who are you looking at? You must want to start something." The kid reaches into his pocket. Suddenly I am chicken-shit scared. I quickly look down, glad this is my stop.

At the vet's office, I can't shake this scared feeling. Mami keeps pressing my shoulder. "Don't worry." The vet gives Isadore the once-over. "Son, your iguana has a case of mouth rot. With some antibiotics, he'll be as good as new."

The question I want to ask somebody is whether I will ever be as good as new.

On the way home, Mami tells me that starting tomorrow, I'll be attending a day camp program at St. Benedict's. It's a community action project and kids do goody-goody stuff like work in a soup kitchen, clean the parks, recycle, and deliver meals to the homebound. What is wrong with this woman? Can't she see I'm a wreck? Well, I've got news for her. I'm not going.

Chapter 9

Just one week, then I don't have to go anymore if I don't like it. That's what Mami said as we walked to St. Benedict's. After camp I was supposed to go to the salon, which is two blocks away from the community center. Did I need her to come pick me up? No. I felt stupid enough making her bring me when most kids probably came by themselves.

In St. Benedict's meeting room, there are dozens of metal folding chairs stacked in a corner. As the kids come in, they grab one and sit by their buddies. I sit alone, hidden behind a column. I'm watching Brother Bill, the guy who heads this community action junk, make the rounds checking off kids' names on a roster. He's already asked me my name three times. Brother Bill is a Benedictine monk. He's chubby and bald and dresses in a nylon jogging suit and tennis shoes instead of a long robe, rope belt, and leather sandals. I know some of the kids here from the neighborhood. There's Quiet Willy, already looking lost. What! Right behind him, coming through the doors, are Adrian and Sam. This must be some kind of mistake. They must have made a wrong turn somewhere. I can't believe this. Brother Bill is adding their names to the list. Wait up, this community action project has got to be a cover for recruiting wannabe delinquents, 'cause that's what Adrian and Sam are. *Ciao,* St. Benedict's! This is my getting-out-of-here time. See ya.

Later I walked into the salon, and everybody started:

"Look, Enoch's smiling."

"Enoch, *mi hijito,* how was your day?"

"*Sí,* tell us all about camp," Dona Ida said from under the dryer.

Julio was busy lathering a customer's hair. Mami was putting perm rollers on Dona Felicia. As I passed Mami a roller, I announced that I'd worked in the soup kitchen.

"*Qué bueno.*"

"What a good deed."

"Good boy."

I added that I worked next to a homeless guy who I suspect might be a homicidal maniac or worse.

"*Ay!*" Dona Felicia screamed as Mami accidentally yanked her hair.

"*Perdón, perdón.*" Mami shook her head. "Enoch, you and your jokes. End of conversation for now."

Julio stamped his foot. "No fair. Just when the boy's story is getting good. Go on, Enoch. What about this homicidal maniac?"

"Julio!" Mami threw a roller at him, but he swerved and it almost hit the customer on the head. "Enoch!"

Funny how you get blamed for every little thing.

* * *

You know, I was telling the truth about the soup kitchen and the homeless guy. See, just when I was going to leave St. Benedict's, I bumped smack into Carmen. It seems her mother had enrolled her in the camp, too. Was she there to spy on me? Who knows? Carmen had never snitched on me before, but if pressure was applied, I'm sure she'd crack. So much for my getaway. Carmen looked really pleased to see me. She smiled, showing off her metal braces.

"Are you hungry?" she asked, opening her knapsack. It was full of junk food. She couldn't possibly eat all this stuff by herself. I picked out a chocolate snack cake. Brother Bill called order.

"Boys and girls, you'll be working in teams of three or four and rotating shifts. Now, if you have a preference, let me know when I call your name."

Carmen nudged me and said maybe we should form a team. I said I wasn't sure if I was going to stay. I mean I was just checking it out.

From across the auditorium, I could see Adrian and Sam coming toward us.

"We're a team, Enoch! Come on, man." Adrian put his arm around my shoulders. What was this?

Whatever it was, it wasn't friendship. In elementary school, these guys hadn't bothered with me, maybe 'cause Spencer was always watching my back.

Then little Carmen put her hands in her back jean pockets and got up in Adrian's face and said, "Enoch is on my team. Our mothers said we have to be together."

"Fine. That makes four."

Carmen's eyes scanned the room and landed on Quiet Willy, who was scratching his head and nervously looking around.

"Willy has to be with us, too. Our mothers said so."

"Willy? Uh-uh." Sam looked like he was going to spit.

Adrian tightened his grip around my shoulders. "What's it going to be, Enoch?"

"I promised my mom. Sorry."

"Mama's boy." Adrian grinned. "We'll catch you later."

"Count on it, bro." Sam punched my arm like you see football players do. It hurt like crazy.

I told Carmen I owed her big time. She smiled, silver gleaming.

Carmen and I, along with Quiet Willy, were assigned to the soup kitchen crew.

"You're sure you want me on your team?" Quiet Willy kept asking, like he didn't trust us.

"Of course," Carmen said, offering him a bag of chips from her knapsack.

"You guys follow me." A young brother in training, who told us to just call him B. G., took us along a small corridor and down some stairs to the basement. Now, B. G. was built like a Mack truck, huge. I figured the *G* stood for *gigante*. Anyway, Brother Giant led us to the kitchen and took off quickly because he had to get another team of kids situated. Now, adults talk about kids not getting along—let me tell you, no sooner did we get to the soup kitchen than this little man with a wild mustache starts arguing with Brother Bill.

The man shouted, "I quit," and tossed his apron. It landed across Brother Bill's face. No joke. It was pretty funny, only I didn't laugh. I wasn't in the mood. I guess I was still worrying about Adrian and Sam. First thing I noticed about this kitchen was the jumbo-size cans of pork and beans stacked on the counter. I hate pork and beans.

Brother Bill kept saying, "Antonio, be reasonable."

"No, no. I'm sick of your promises. You promise me ground beef so I can make my special meat loaf. But no, no. I get hot dogs! Hot dogs!" Antonio whirled around and faced me. "Does this look like Yankee Stadium?"

I shook my head. It sure didn't look like Yankee Stadium. Then Antonio stormed out of the kitchen, with Brother Bill in hot pursuit.

Now this scene didn't faze the adult volunteers working in the soup kitchen. They kept right on doing their own thing. An old man was washing carrots and heads of cabbage, while two ladies scraped the skin off the carrots so another man could pass the carrots and the cabbage through the food processor. In the corner by the sink, a scraggly-looking man with long hair tied back in a ponytail was filling a huge pot with water. Our eyes met for a second. I knew right away this was the crazy bum I see all the time in Poe Park.

Brother Bill came back. His face was beet red and sweaty. I think I heard him mutter a curse word. As he rolled up the sleeves of his jogging suit, he said, "Well, folks, in less than two hours, some of God's hungriest will be walking through those cafeteria doors expecting a meal. Maybe their only meal for the day. So let's get busy."

"Wow." Carmen elbowed me and Quiet Willy, who was more quiet than usual. Brother Bill suddenly became the general of the soup kitchen, and we were all soldiers. Let me tell you, I didn't like it one bit. I liked it even less when Brother Bill ordered me to help Ed, the bum, boil the hot dogs.

So I played nice. You can't get aggressive with unstable people. That'll just set them off. When I said carefully, "Hi, I'm Enoch. What do you want me to do?" Ed looked at me like I was a banana brain.

"Who named you?"

I said my mom. She got it out of a name book.

"You adopted?"

I shook my head.

"Weird name. It fits you, though." Ed smiled.

I stood there wondering if I had just been insulted, while Ed went into the freezer and brought back a bag of hot dogs and threw it on the counter. Then he turned back to go to the freezer again. I followed him. He grabbed another bag and I went to grab one, too. Simple. Right? They pack about a hundred or more hot dogs in these bags. I knocked over everything just trying to put it on the counter. I felt like every single eye in that kitchen was focused on me. Everybody's eyes except Ed's. He was busy ripping open the plastic bags.

"Come on, kid. This is Yankee Stadium. We got to boil these wieners for the Bronx Bombers." Ed winked, the kind of wink that made you feel like you were part of something.

While the hot dogs were boiling, I worked with some other kids wiping the tops of the long wooden tables and benches in the cafeteria. A nice volunteer lady with blond dreadlocks gave us hot dogs and apple juice. I put sauerkraut and mustard on my hot dog. We could take another if we wanted. Hmm. Tasty. The juice was cold and refreshing.

"I think I am going to like this," Quiet Willy muttered between bites.

The lady said, "What, the hot dogs or camp?"

Quiet Willy smiled.

When the doors opened, I couldn't believe my eyes. I had never seen so many street people in one place before. One by one, they each took a tray and proceeded down the food line—hot dogs, pork and beans, cole slaw, and applesauce. The broccoli-stuffed baked potatoes were for the vegetarians.

Brother Bill told us to get upstairs for game time. As I left, I saw an old woman wrap her hot dog in a napkin, maybe for later, maybe for someone else.

Back in the meeting room, the metal chairs had been folded away. Some kids were practicing flips on the mats lined up against the wall. On the other wall a basketball game was in progress. Here and there kids were playing board games, jumping rope, and generally acting stupid. B. G. blew the whistle every time he saw somebody break the big game-time rule: NO CHASING GAMES. Despite his size, I could tell B. G. was afraid of kids, afraid they'd take advantage. So he comes on too strong. I told this to Carmen. She agreed.

Believe it or not, somewhere in her knapsack stocked like a corner bodega, Carmen had tucked away a jump rope. Slowly, inch by inch, she fished it out. Quiet Willy was sitting cross-legged on a mat, looking at a science magazine. Tomorrow I'll definitely be prepared. I'll bring something to pass the boring time away. I looked all around for Adrian and Sam, not because I wanted to find them. I just didn't want them sneaking up on me. For now, though, the coast was clear. They were probably still outdoors with the group, delivering food to the homebound. *Ay,* I wouldn't open my door to those guys. They're probably taking notes so someday they can come back and steal. I was going to tell this to Carmen, but she was already spinning and hopping through double-Dutch hoops. If Spencer was here, we would have ambushed that rope. We could step a mean double Dutch and not look like girls. B. G. motioned to Quiet Willy and me to join the basketball game that was already going on. I didn't have anything better to do. Quiet Willy stayed reading his magazine. I don't think he knows how to play.

Julio just left. Mami invited him to have dinner. It was overdue. Mami wanted to do something to thank Julio for his work at the salon and welcome him to the neighborhood. A few weeks ago he rented a studio near Fordham Road. It's his first apartment. Julio told us his parents kicked him out of the house when he was fifteen. He's been on his own ever since. *Imaginate.* Thank goodness, a friend's grandmother took him under her wing. She taught him all about styling hair. Julio survived by getting little jobs in salons. He landed with Mami on the day her regular stylist, Ivonne, left to open her own beauty parlor in Queens. Up went the HELP WANTED sign and in walked this skinny kid. Mami said, "*Ay, bendito,* let's give him a chance." It was a matter of *destino.* The kid has a natural flair with the hair and a good disposition. Mami says Julio will be a stylist for the celebs one day, but for now she is encouraging him to get his GED. I figure Julio is sixteen or seventeen years old.

Chapter 10

Sometimes I think, when people say sweet things, it's best to retreat with fast feet. Or at the very least get your back up, because something usually follows that sweet thing, and it's not sweet.

"*Buenos días, mi cielo.* My darling boy. *Te quiero tanto.* Love you so." Mami hugged me this morning. She brought out a box of my favorite cereal, the one with all the sugar that I get to eat once in a while.

"Did you sleep well?"

"Hmmm."

Mami started talking about life. Life is funny, full of surprises. Wouldn't you know, my half brother, Miguel, is coming to stay with us for the rest of the summer. Mami poured milk into my cereal bowl. What, Ma? At first I thought I hadn't heard right. Miguel is my mother's son from her first marriage, which ended in divorce. Mami was really young, so Miguel went to live with his father's relatives in Puerto Rico. When Mami remarried, she asked for Miguel to join her, but the family refused. I met Miguel once. I'm not saying he's bad, but my memory of him is not too cool. It was a summer night. I was chilling with Mami on my grandfather's porch *en la isla*. We were listening to the frogs going *coqui-coqui* when a whole group of noisy people paid us a visit. They filled up the porch. They were all grown-ups except for this boy. Mami was crying and fussing over him. Then she said, "Enoch, come here and kiss your brother, Miguel." Just like that. After a while, the grown-ups went inside the house to talk. I was left alone with Miguel. As we sat on the porch steps, I watched as he took out a slingshot, gathered some pebbles, and aimed them one by one at the bushes where the frogs were. Maybe

Miguel wasn't aiming at the frogs. I don't know, but I'm keeping Isadore away from him.

Over the years, I found that if I mentioned Miguel, Mami would get weepy, so I didn't speak about my brother, not even to ask what she was putting in packages she sent him the first week of every month.

"Enoch, please understand. Your brother needs me." Mami ran her hand over my head. Sounded like a problem walking into my life. I knew this had something to do with the call Mami got late last night. I heard her talking in hushed tones in Spanish for a long time.

Carmen is at the door. We're walking together to St. Benedict's. Her idea.

During game time on the second day of camp, I found out what Adrian and Sam want with me. It's like—Hey, Eno, too bad about Spencer. You two were tight. Word is you were next to him when it all came down. Yeah, tell us. Did you see the bullet hole? Was his chest wide open with guts and blood all over? Were his eyes open or closed?

My body started shaking all over. Couldn't stop it. All I could do was run. I ran out of St. Benedict's and kept on going until I got to Poe Park. The last time I had been there was when I got the news about Spencer. I sat on a bench until I could calm down enough to go home. I was glad that tomorrow was Saturday. No camp.

The next day I lay in bed planning out my day. I wasn't leaving the apartment, or the bed for that matter. Well, maybe just to get a box of cereal and the television remote. Then the phone rang. It was Brother Bill. He had called yesterday, but I erased his message from the answering machine.

Before I could think up an excuse for leaving camp without permission, Mami was beside my bed. She asked if something happened at camp yesterday and did I want to talk about it. I said, "No! Leave me alone." Which was kind of rude, plus I said it nasty. You know Mami flipped.

"Mira, muchacho!"

Even though she is not a hitting woman, I hopped out of arm's reach.

"That does it. Get dressed—you're going to come and help me at the salon. I'm not leaving you to spend your entire day in front of the TV."

I could kick myself. Instead of "Leave me alone," I should have said, "*Mamita linda,* beautiful Mami, I don't want to talk about it now, *por favor.* Thank you for asking."

All day long my job at the salon was to maintain a clean establishment. Tidying up magazines. Gathering dirty towels. Sweeping the floor. Sometimes I would be sent on a extra-special top-priority errand like getting a newspaper, coffee, or *cuchifrito,* a yucca fried fritter, for a customer.

Boring.

I don't think Mami realizes that she's messing up my head by making me listen to ladies' beauty parlor talk. Sweeping up the hair, all I hear is "*Ay, m'ija,* let me tell you about that *hombre.*"

The guys really get dissed in my mom's salon. If a guy comes in to get his hair cut, the conversation turns to kids. Kids get dissed worse than guys. It's awful.

Mami said that after work we're all going to Fordham Road to buy a cot for Miguel to sleep on. He's going to be sleeping in my room. Why not the living room? Why my room?

Diablo! Someone turned on the fan, and now the hair I swept up is flying all over the place.

After work Mami and Julio spent forever trying to figure out what cot to buy. You ask me, one cot is the same as another. Finally they decided on one. It took a while to get a taxi driver who didn't mind hauling the cot in his trunk. Then Julio and I had to carry the cot up the stairs 'cause the elevator was out of order. Let me tell you, if I worked for a moving company with Julio, I'd go crazy. He complains about every little thing. "*Ay!* Be careful! That's my finger. *Ay!* I can't see. Go faster. Go slower." Forget it. At any rate, by nine o'clock I was in bed.

Bright and early Sunday morning I accompanied Mami to church. Although I didn't want to, I volunteered. It's all part of my plan. See, tonight I'm going to tell Mami I'm not returning to camp. I just can't go back there. Adrian and Sam are going to keep after me. I know it.

The priest talked about God loving little kids best of all. Yeah, right.

On the way home, Mami and I stopped at the bakery. She asked me what pastries I think Miguel would like. How would I know? Like I said, I only met him once. I told Mami to get all the ones I like.

We crossed the street, I hinted about camp, and Mami reminded me that I promised to stick it out for a week, at least. I began to tell her about Adrian and Sam, but Spencer's grandmother, Mrs. Bandy, walked by us. She was dragging a small empty shopping cart. Mami stopped her and they chatted for a few minutes. Mrs. Bandy said she was considering moving to New Jersey. Her social worker said she could get her affordable housing there.

"It will be hard to leave the neighborhood. I'll feel like I am leaving Spencer behind." Mrs. Bandy sniffled. "But for the sake of the other boys, I would do anything."

I stood nearby, wishing the cracks in the pavement would open enough to let me slip through. Before she left, Mrs. Bandy smiled and touched my cheek. I noticed how tired she looked. She must have lost ten pounds or more, and her hair is almost completely gray. It didn't use to be like that. Seeing Mrs. Bandy reminded me how much I miss her grandson.

Sometimes I catch myself thinking about Spence like he's not gone. If I hear a song, I think, Wow, my buddy would really like this beat. I keep waiting to tell him my best jokes, like he is somewhere far away and coming back any day now. Or I see Spencer walking down the street, but it's not him, just some kid that looks like him.

Sometimes I want to forget. I mean, offer me a pill that would erase Spencer from my thoughts and I'd take it. Swallow it in a sec. No. How could I do that? *Ay,* Spence, you must be looking at me from wherever you're at, thinking that I'm some kind of lousy friend. Sorry, bro. *Sorry* doesn't come close.

Chapter 11

Nightmare! I woke up in the morning and found this teenage boy sleeping in the cot next to my bed. Only it wasn't a dream.

I jumped out of bed and tripped over a suitcase. My ankle got caught in the straps. I came crashing to the floor. "Shh!" Mami opened the bedroom door. "You'll wake your brother. He caught an earlier flight. Now, Enoch, please try to be quiet while you get ready."

I can tell you one thing about my brother, Miguel. He's a sound sleeper. There is so much racket in the street this morning. Cars honking. Dogs barking. Jackhammer hammering. Add to the mix some girl shouting for somebody to throw down the keys, and a boom box blasting a rapper's song about how bad he wants it.

You know what? Miguel scrunches up his mouth like Mami when he's asleep. He's way taller than I thought he'd be. Stretched out lengthwise, he just about fits the cot. I'm not giving up my bed. No way. Mami says Miguel's seventeen, but he looks older. Yeah. He has an impressive tattoo of a crucifix on his biceps.

I'm not the only one checking out Miguel. Isadore is clinging on to the side of the cot near Miguel's pillow.

"Hey, Izzy! Don't worry. I'm not leaving you in strange hands. That's a promise. You're going to camp."

I am true to my word. Isadore went to camp. I've got the smooth moves of some kind of secret agent. I emptied out my backpack and put Isadore inside. Just so he could breathe, I left the bag a little open. Then I sneaked Isadore past Mami, Brother Bill, and the kids at camp, except Carmen, Quiet Willy, and Ed. Carmen knew 'cause I told her the minute she showed up at my door in the morning. Quiet Willy knew 'cause he's part of our team. He's quiet, so a secret stays with him. Ed, well, he saw me in the stairwell near the soup kitchen talking into my backpack. He asked me why I wasn't upstairs with the rest of the kids. He sounded like a teacher. I thought, That's it. This guy was going to tell on me. I pulled Isadore out. You know what? Ed may be a bum, but he is cool. He actually asked to hold Isadore and he said his markings were beautiful. What's more, he knows a thing or two about iguanas. Then he told me there was an aluminum tub in the utility closet near the pantry. Most people didn't use that closet 'cause the slop sink didn't work. Izzy could stay there. Only thing is we needed something on top of the tub to keep him penned in. Didn't somebody just throw a bunch of old window screens in the garbage bin? Together Ed and I set up a cozy place for Izzy to hang out while I was at camp. Whenever I wanted to, I could go check up on him and bring him some food scraps.

Another good thing, Adrian is a no-show at camp, and Sam didn't come near me all day.

Pretty decent day—except for Miguel. Just as I suspected. He's a jerk. One day and he is already bossing me around.

"*Hermanito, deme un baso de agua.*" Get me a glass of water. Miguel mostly talks in Spanish, but he knows English. He just speaks it with a heavy accent.

"*Gracias,*" he said when I slammed the glass of water down next to his dinner plate.

Mami shot me a look. She was a nervous wreck all evening. I had never seen her this way.

Miguel kept right on eating. All night there was this bold half-smile on his lips, as if he found everything amusing. His leg was bobbing up and down. His palms drummed on the table. He was like these people that can't sit still for too long. I studied his every move like he was an alien that landed in my world. I watched as he small-talked with Mami about *la isla.* I couldn't help but notice, when he and Mami sat side by side, that he looks more like her than I do.

After dinner Mami said she bought all the ingredients for me to fix everybody ice-cream sundaes. Just don't make a mess. I'm like the mad scientist of sundaes. My concoctions are awesome—fresh fruit, walnuts, chocolate chips, coconut flakes, fudge syrup, whipped cream, and maraschino cherries—oh yeah, and some ice cream, too. Last Christmas Mami gave me a set of sundae dishes and spoons. Fancy. Spence loved my sundaes.

"Come on, Enoch. *Por favor.*" I knew Mami wanted some time alone with Miguel.

I got busy making sundaes. I added extra coconut and a banana to Miguel's. Mami asked for a mango sundae, like it was a special request. *No problema.* When I handed Miguel his sundae, he opened his eyes wide. Never in my life have I seen anyone attack a sundae like Miguel. *Slurp. Slurp.* All done! Suddenly he was on his feet. He stretched out his arms. "*Necesito aire.* You want to go outside with me, *hermanito?*"

What? It was a little past nine o'clock at night.

"He has camp tomorrow," Mami said quickly.

"You don't trust me."

Mami hesitated. "This neighborhood is *caliente.*"

"Once around the block. I'll take good care of him."

I expected Mami to protest, but she gave in.

As we walked, Miguel was silent. He was like a night dweller surveying a new territory. A group of teenagers filled the sidewalk. When Miguel and I passed among them, I could feel their stares. Miguel put his hand on my shoulder and guided me across the street.

"*Hermanito,* don't ever show you are afraid. Even if you are."

"Shouldn't we get back? Mami will worry."

"What a baby." Miguel smiled. "You have a lot to learn."

The next morning Isadore walked into my knapsack. I think he likes the utility closet at St. Benedict's. Miguel woke up early. He was singing in the shower, belting it out in Spanish like he thought he had a voice. Please.

I banged on the bathroom door. "Hey, I have to pee." Mami told me to stop making such a fuss and hold it for a minute. "Hold it?" I said. "I'm going to explode. I have to pee now!"

The bathroom door swung open. Miguel was standing there in a towel and he had a glob of shaving cream on his face.

"Come in, *hermanito.*" He smiled, parked himself in front of the bathroom mirror, and continued shaving. *Adiós,* privacy!

On our way to camp, Carmen told me she can't believe how cute my brother Miguel is. Wasn't it funny how Miguel called her my "little girlfriend"? Yeah, really funny. We stopped at Tedoro's bodega. I've been a customer of Tedoro's ever since I can remember. He treats kids kind of lousy, but he's got the best candy selection in the neighborhood. His wife makes the best homemade candy too. Her *dulce de coco* can't be beat. So kids put up with Tedoro's grouchiness and the sideways look he gives them through his eyeglasses. Tedoro has the thickest lenses I've ever seen.

Today I got a chocolate bar and bubble gum. Carmen got a bunch of stuff—too much. She won't eat even half of it. She'll give it away. I think Carmen is too nice sometimes.

As we leave the bodega, Carmen holds out a fistful of nickel candy. "Want some, Enoch?" I don't remember her paying for those. Maybe she did and I wasn't looking.

Adrian is a no-show again!

And yeah, I discovered that Ed has problems. No kidding. Quiet Willy, Carmen, and I came down early to the soup kitchen so we could get Isadore settled, and there was Ed scribbling in a notebook. He didn't notice us at first. Writing in a notebook? No biggie. Now, talking to it as if he expected a reply—well . . .

"Annie, I don't want to argue with you. I have so many papers to write. Please don't cry. I do want the baby. Stop! Things will get better, I promise. I promise. I promise."

There was a strong smell of liquor in the air. Ed looked at us. He closed his notebook and rubbed his eyes.

"How's everybody, and I mean everybody, including iguanas, doing this morning?"

While we were wiping down tables, Quiet Willy told me that his father drinks too much and that's why his mother goes to church, night and day. She is trying to save him.

"But you know, Enoch, you can't save people who don't want to be saved." Quiet Willy sounded like an old man.

"You think Ed wants to be saved?"

Quiet Willy shook his head. We wiped a couple more tables.

"Hey, Willy, how come you are always so quiet?" I said finally.

"Who's quiet?"

"You."

Willy smiled. "Quiet people rule the world."

I believe it. One day people will say, *oye,* remember that quiet kid? He is the head of the FBI or something. Who's his number one agent? Enoch Morales. Ha. Ha. Ha.

Slow afternoon. I taught Quiet Willy some of my smooth moves with a basketball. If you're going to rule the world, you got to rule the court. Quiet Willy learns fast. Carmen jumped in with her friend Marisol. Carmen can play because her dad taught her. Marisol said she plays with her older sister, who's on a team. Together we messed around and passed the time okay.

At the end of the day, I stopped by the salon. Julio was sitting in a swivel seat enjoying a glass of *limonada.* Mami was out getting some items she needed from the beauty supply store.

"I met Miguel." Julio narrowed his eyes. "He got his hair cut this morning. Boy, did he need it."

"Where is he now?"

"*Ay*, who knows. I think he's checking out the neighborhood or something. Maybe he wants the neighborhood to check him out. Look what just flew in from P.R."

I poured myself a glass of *limonada* and sat in the swivel seat beside Julio.

"Mami told you about Miguel?" I asked like I didn't care. "Did she tell about the problems he had in Puerto Rico?"

"I promised Lourdes I wouldn't tell."

"Come on. I live with him now. I ought to know. We sleep in the same room."

"Watch your back."

"What? Did he stab somebody?"

Julio gave me a meaningful look.

"*Tranquilo.* I am not exactly saying he stabbed anybody. It's the lifestyle. Let's just say that in the circles Miguel was associated with, stabbings are a possibility."

"Miguel was in a gang?"

"I didn't tell you that."

Julio can't hold a secret for nothing. I just had to keep working him. It was obviously going to take several sessions.

I could see Mami heading up the street. I had time for only one more question.

"But Miguel's going back in September. Right?"

Julio rolled his eyes.

Chapter 12

Bad day for iguanas. Isadore is banned from St. Benedict's for life. Don't ask me how, but he got out of the utility closet and wound up in a bag of onions. When one of the volunteers went to grab an onion, yow, everybody was screaming like Godzilla was loose and running wild in St. Benedict's soup kitchen. Poor Isadore, he didn't know which way to go with the brooms and spatulas slamming down hard around him. I thought they were going to kill him. Then Quiet Willy let out a bone-chilling scream: "Fire! Fire!"

When everybody turned, I threw myself down on the floor and nabbed Isadore as he headed under the dishwasher. Ed was jumping up and down, cheering like I had scored a touchdown or something. That's when Brother Bill and his sidekick, B. G., came on the scene. They were not amused. Brother Bill made me promise to never bring Isadore back.

"Never, ever, Enoch."

"Okay, okay."

From now on, Quiet Willy is Willy. Period. Yesterday I told him that we should take our bicycles for a spin over the weekend. Willy said okay, only afterward he had to go to prayer service with his mom. *Ay!*

It's a beautiful day for a bike ride. Willy and I are zipping through Poe Park laughing like *loco.* I am telling him he ought to try out for horror movies with that scream of his, when who should I spot sitting on a bench surrounded by Spencer's cousin Dougie and his crew, but Miguel. Can you believe that everybody is hanging on to his every word as if he has something important to say?

*   *   *

Now—what should I do? Should I tell Mami? After dinner Miguel fixes Mami's old radio. Mami keeps commenting how good he is with his hands. Yeah, good for fighting and who knows what else. I had to get more information from Julio. Miguel winks at me.

"Why is my baby brother so serious?"

Mami touches my cheek. "This hasn't been an easy summer for Enoch. You know I told you."

"Right. Maybe we could have a brother-to-brother talk about things sometime." Miguel lunges at me playfully. "I bet you don't even know how to wrestle."

What he doesn't know is I used to wrestle with Spencer all the time.

I leap on Miguel. We tangle on the floor. You figure Miguel would pin me down one-two-three. Instead, he shows me how not to get pinned. He's not being gentle with me and he's not being rough. He's more like a coach. "That's right, *hermanito*—be quick and slippery. Just like that. Just like that. *Epa!*"

I don't know where Mami got the camera, but she is snapping away like a sports photographer.

"Don't break anything, boys." I wonder if she is talking about bones or furniture.

The wrestling bout was cool, but Miguel is not fooling me. I know the deal. Mami should know it too, but she looks so happy.

Ding-ding. Sunday morning I woke up just as Miguel sat up on his cot. Before he could say *hermanito,* I was on my feet, rushing for the bathroom. I heard Miguel's deep laugh. The smell of bacon filled the air. Mami must have put some on to sizzle in a pan just to speed my morning hygiene routine. I took a quick shower. Mami also had pancakes on the griddle, something she usually does only on Sunday mornings. When I got to the bedroom, Miguel was on the floor, doing push-ups. He was only wearing shorts. I had to step all over him to get my stuff.

"Hermanito," Miguel said, "you got to build some muscles if you want to pin people down."

Whatever. While I tied my sneakers, I watched Miguel's back muscles press in and out. He kind of reminded me of a boxer getting ready for a match. Spence told me once about Dougie's initiation into

93

Firearms. Crew members form a circle around a new recruit and he has to fight his way out. Miguel looked like he could hold his own in a fight one-on-one, but against a pack—those were losers' odds. He was setting himself up.

"I saw you yesterday hanging out with Firearms."

Miguel kept on doing his push-ups and I kept on talking.

"This isn't P.R. You don't know what you're getting into. These gangs do bad things. They mess up the neighborhood. They hurt people. So watch out."

Miguel stood up. "*Hermanito,* you have all the answers. You don't know anything."

"I do know. My friend was killed by some kids playing with a gun."

"That's different. I am just getting by in the only way I know how. I didn't have Mami with me like you do. Don't worry, I'll be a cool guest."

"Mami loves you a lot."

"I guess so, but she gave me up, didn't she?"

"She had to."

"I have to do what I have to do."

Ay, cabeza dura. It is so frustrating talking to hardheaded people.

Just then Mami called, "Boys, food is on the table."

After breakfast Miriam came by and drove us to Bear Mountain. Miguel and I sat silently in the backseat. Mami kept turning around to ask us if everything was all right. Fine. Miriam was preoccupied, too. Maybe she was thinking about Carmen, who was visiting her stepfather in New Jersey for a couple of days. We could have really used Carmen to liven up this ride. Finally Mami turned on the radio. Spanish music never sounded so sweet. We all started singing to the songs we knew. Miguel and Mami sang the harmony, while Miriam and I did the backup. We were the Latin groove on the move.

The day turned out to be perfectly *perfecto*. When we got to Bear Mountain, we went straight to the pond, where we rented pedal-it-yourself boats. Miguel and I got in one, Mami and Miriam in the other. Now Miguel and I pedaled circles around the rest of the boats. We would have won a race if there was one. Boy, it was fun. Afterward, we hiked a bit. Miguel told me about El Yunque, the rain forest in Puerto Rico. I want to go there someday. Isadore would love it!

On the way home, the traffic was heavy. I fell asleep. I dreamed I was pedaling a boat in the Caribbean Sea. Funny, it wasn't Miguel pedaling beside me but Spencer. My buddy was so happy.

Chapter 13

There is blood on my white T-shirt and it's not mine. See, this is what happened. Adrian came back. Sam and him saw me and instantly took up where they left off.

It was game time. I was minding my business, just sitting on the mat with Willy. He was showing me a card trick. Not a baby card trick, either. A Las Vegas–style trick, with subtle hand moves and fancy shuffling. Willy said that his mom had taught it to him. What? Yep, his mom, the one who is always at prayer services. *Increíble.* Anyway, Willy was very patiently showing me the steps, when Adrian and Sam threw themselves plop down on the mat next to us.

Adrian started talking loud. "Hey, Sam, didn't you figure that Enoch and Spencer were like brothers or something?"

"Yeah. Tighter than tight," Sam answered Adrian as if he were reading a script.

"Word." Adrian shook his head in disappointment. "But now I see Enoch wasn't Spencer's true friend. A true friend would know what Spencer was all about. Sure would."

Sam echoed, "Sure would."

"Enoch, don't listen to them," Willy whispered. "They are trying to mess with you." Spencer would have said the same thing to me if he was around. So I tried my best to ignore them. B. G. wanted us to play basketball. Willy said no. He stayed on the mat perfecting his card trick. I should have stayed with him.

I was on the team opposite Adrian and Sam. As I was making a pass, Adrian was on my back.

"Sam, I think it's pretty funny, if you ask me. Enoch here hasn't a clue. Should we tell him? Everyone knows."

I tried to lose Adrian.

Sam made an attempt to swipe the ball. "Go ahead. Tell him."

"Enoch, Spencer was drug running. Just what you expect from a crack baby."

"Liar!" I yelled as I turned and slammed the ball hard into Adrian's stomach. We were on the floor. Kids tried to separate us. A whistle blew. But I wasn't ready to stop. This fight was just starting. I was going to make Adrian eat his words. Knock the words back into him. Make him sorry he ever said Spencer's name. Oh, yeah. When B. G. pulled me off Adrian, I was punching the air. Adrian was crying, his lip all bloody.

"Watch your back, Enoch! That's all I'm telling you. Watch your back!"

B. G. escorted us to Brother Bill's office. Adrian got to tell his side of the story first. I sat outside on the bench, not caring whether I got expelled from camp or not.

"What happened, son?" Brother Bill kept asking when it was my turn. Only I wasn't saying a word. My fists were still clenched. "Speak to me." Brother Bill tried to look in my eyes. "Adrian says you attacked him without provocation. Is that true? This is not like you, Enoch. What's going on?" I wanted to say, "What's going on is that the old Enoch is dead. This is the new Enoch. Get used to it."

Mami came into the office. She was out of breath. You can tell she dropped everything and came running. She still had on her blue work smock, and there was a smudge of hair color on her cheek. Brother Bill told me to wait outside. I could hear Mami apologizing for my behavior. I wished she'd stop.

Brother Bill said I should go home with Mami. The silent walk to the salon was like stepping on an eggshell pavement. Occasionally, I caught Mami looking at me. When she wasn't paying attention, I looked at her. I was trying to read her face. I bet she was angry. Disappointed. Tired. Probably all of the above. I was just glad for the silence.

"Por fin!" Julio rushed over to us as we entered. "Lourdes, the three o'clock is here. The three-thirty came early. The two o'clock came late. This customer walked in off the street. It's not good to turn business away. What a day for problems!"

Mami rolled up her sleeves. "Enoch. We will talk later."

"Fighting is so so so stupid." Julio clicked his teeth.

The next thing you know, Mami was mixing hair color in the back and Julio was washing the three o'clock's hair.

I thought about Spencer and lies.

We got home late. I went straight to my room.

"Enoch?" Mami knelt by the bed, soothing my back.

I didn't tell Mami I had to defend Spencer's honor. The only thing I would tell her about the fight was that Adrian started it.

"How did he start it, *papito*?"

No response.

"I wish I could make the hurt go away, like when you were a baby. *Sana, sana, colita de rana. Si no sanas hoy, sanaras mañana.* Remember?"

No response. Heal, heal, little frog's tail. If you don't heal today, you'll heal tomorrow.

"You know you can talk to me."

Eyes closed. No response.

"Psst. Enoch. It's Miguel. Wake up. Mami told me you had a fight. If you tell me who, I'll take care of when and where. Only kidding. You have to fight your own battles. Like a man. Look at me." Through my sleepy eyes, I could see Miguel on his cot flexing his biceps like Mr. Universe.

"Miguel?"

"What?"

"Has Dougie ever talked about Spencer?"

"A little."

"Has he told you if Spencer ever—did bad things for him?"

"*Hermanito.* Look at the time! I can't keep my eyes open. *Buenas noches.* Hey, leave the fighting to me."

Spencer wouldn't be involved in drugs. He hated that junk. He hated what it did to his mother. I know. But what if? Spence. You had that money. I have to know for sure, buddy. I have to talk to Dougie. I can always find him hanging out in Poe Park.

*　　*　　*

The next day Mami didn't wake me up. I wondered if Brother Bill called and said he didn't want any troublemaking kids at St. Benedict's camp. I wouldn't blame him.

Nobody is home. Miguel's cot is closed, his bed linen neatly folded on top. There is a note on the fridge: *Enoch: Heat up breakfast and meet me at the salon. Love, Mami.* She even drew a heart with a happy face.

I am going to Poe Park to get the answers I need. I'll wait there for as long as it takes.

Chapter 14

There's this world I never saw before. Maybe I saw it, but I didn't ever think that it had anything to do with me. I always felt protected. Now it's different.

But I'm not afraid anymore 'cause I don't care. I don't care what happens from this point on—if I live, if I die. I don't care. Kill me. Shoot me. Throw me in a ditch. I feel sorry for Mami. I love her very much. But I don't care anymore. I don't.

Dougie said Spencer was the best little runner he ever had.

It's nighttime. I can't sleep. I just had a dream I was standing in front of the fire hydrant on the hottest summer day. Where the sprinkler cap used to be was this gaping hole, bone dry. I knelt down and looked into it, only it wasn't shaped like a hydrant anymore. It was shaped like a huge .38 gun. As I was looking down its barrel, I felt a hand on my shoulder. It was Spencer. That's when I woke up.

There's sweat running down my body. Miguel isn't in his bed. The window screen is loose. He must have sneaked down the fire escape. This brother of mine has the right idea. I secured the screen and waved see-ya to Isadore.

I'd never been out on the street alone past 10 P.M. When they say on TV, "It's 10 P.M. Do you know where your children are?" I used to say, "Right here on the couch."

Well, no more. I went roaming, and in my neighborhood, well, that's like asking for it. What was I asking for? I don't know. When a gang of stray cats ran by me, I don't know who was more scared, me or the cats.

Truth is, I spent most of the time hiding in and out of shadows. You know what happens to the streets in the night? They become haunted. It's like an evil board game, only real. Two steps forward, you hear a bottle breaking in the distance. A couple steps back, and you see what looks like a dark figure lurking in the alley. The only thing you can do is run. Run to the nearest place you know. For me, that's Poe Park.

There were people in Poe Park. Not a lot but some. A guy and a lady arguing, a group of teenagers in the rotunda laughing and carrying on, and a kid on a skateboard doing zigzags down the Grand Concourse.

I was still jumpy. Just as I got ready to sit on a bench facing the Concourse, I noticed this guy sprawled out there. Something about him looked familiar. I got up close to him. It was dark, even though the street lamps illuminated the park. The guy sprang up like a mummy from a crypt. Oh, Ma. I sure was glad when I recognized Ed's face.

"Enoch? What are you doing here?"

"I couldn't sleep."

Ed smiled. "I know what you mean."

"So this is where you stay?"

"What?"

"This is your home." I motioned to Poe Park around us.

Ed nodded.

"Aren't you afraid someone will hurt you?"

"People mostly leave me alone. If they don't, I act a little crazy to make them want to leave me alone."

"Maybe I ought to try that."

"Enoch, I wouldn't recommend it. Because, look around. This is a hard life. Bad things can happen."

"Bad things happen anyway, you know. My friend died. Right across the street at the fire hydrant. Shot dead. He was my best buddy."

"I am truly sorry." I knew Ed wasn't saying sorry to be polite. He meant it.

Though I hadn't intended on telling him any of this, I kept going. I told Ed all about Adrian and Sam. About Spencer's drug running and how it turns out that I didn't know who my friend was after all. Ed listened. After I finished, we sat in silence watching the cars go up and down the Concourse. There was slow, steady traffic. The *whoosh* of the tires passing by made me sleepy. "Let's take you home, Enoch." Ed slapped my knee.

On the way, we spotted a stray cat sitting on a garbage can. Maybe he was part of the little gang of cats that frightened me earlier. This cat was a mean, mangy-looking mess. He had lost patches of fur, a piece of his ear, and I think an eye. Ed told me the cat reminded him of a scary story. He asked me if I liked scary stories. Yeah, you know I do! Ed told me about a black cat that couldn't be done in by its evil master even after the guy murdered his wife. It was way gruesome. I liked it. Especially the part when the black cat gets even!

Up the fire escape I went, home before Miguel.

I'm a light sleeper, and when Miguel came in about six o'clock in the morning, so long, *siesta*. Miguel was hoisting a thirty-gallon glass tank through the window into the room. He was really happy. He said the tank was for Isadore. He told me he found it in the trash. Wasn't it in good condition? As he pulled off his shirt, he told me that later he would show me how to set up the tank with a hiding box and lamp, all the extras. No more punch bowl. Isadore was going to be living in style, a condominium with a heating unit.

"Go back to sleep, *hermanito*. You look like you've been up all night." Miguel laughed. Then he lay back on his cot and was zonked out in seconds. Isadore was perched on the side of the punch bowl looking at the tank. I think he knew it was his.

Later Willy called. He said camp was the same-old same-old. Carmen was back. All the kids were still talking about how I beat Adrian. Oh, the soup kitchen staff was asking for me. When was I coming back?

I figured being at camp was better than sitting around thinking, so I asked Mami if I could go back to St. Benedict's. She said I could if I wanted to. Brother Bill didn't expel me. "Just don't get into any more fights, Enoch—please." Okay. I promised. It didn't feel good to lie.

I slammed into Carmen as she came charging out of Tedoro's bodega. Tedoro was screaming after her. "Get out, you little thief, and don't come back! I know your mother!" Carmen took one look at me and ran.

"What's the matter?" I asked Tedoro.

"What's the matter is that your little friend, the

daughter of a police officer, has been robbing me. I don't see so good, but today I catch her stuffing her bag. And she doesn't pay. Tell her she's lucky I don't tell her mother."

I could imagine Miriam in her patrol car getting the call. Talk about big-time trouble. I told myself not to get involved. Why should I?

Anyway, Carmen was a no-show at camp. Sam and Adrian just eyeballed me. Willy said they were planning to jump me. Try it. Ed was in bad shape, really soused. He kept on repeating that poem about Annabel Lee. Finally Brother Bill had to take him aside to talk to him. Hey, what do I care? It's nice Ed walked me home last night, but he's nothing to me.

After camp I rode my bike. I stopped outside Carmen's building, thinking over the reasons why I should keep on moving and not bother with her. So Carmen's shoplifting. Not your problem, Enoch. Shoplifting. What is going on with this girl? Face it, Enoch. You don't know what Carmen's going through. Like you didn't know about—whatever.

I figured I'd just drop by and say hi. What harm is there in hi? Right? Wrong.

I pressed on the intercom button downstairs.

Scratchy static. I could hardly make out Carmen's voice.

"Who is it?" she said.

"It's Enoch."

"Who?"

I said, "It's me." She asked who again and again—until I shouted into the intercom so loud the people in the street stopped and looked my way. I was starting to feel like this was a bad idea, when Carmen came to the downstairs door. Right off it was, "Enoch, what do you want?"

"Hey," I said. "It's not every day you get run out of a store for shoplifting. Don't you feel bad about it? Stealing is wrong."

"You're not my father."

"No kidding. I don't look a thing like him."

Carmen flipped. "Don't talk about my father. Just because he's not around doesn't mean he doesn't care about me."

"I didn't bring him up—you did."

"Oh, shut up!" Carmen turned away. I could see she was crying. *Ay*, this was too much. My fault. I should have gone easy on her.

"Ah, sorry, Carmen. I'm *bruto* through and through. Come out. Climb on the handlebars of my bike and I'll give you a ride."

As we breezed through the streets, I kept thinking that the last person I let ride on my bike was Spencer. That was so long ago.

At Poe Park we bought coconut ices and chilled on the bench. Carmen told me that her mom was working overtime at the precinct. Her dad was making a new life for himself with this lady Carmen didn't like. Sometimes Carmen felt like nobody was around. I told her that she ought to drop by the salon more often. My mom was crazy about her, and Julio, man, he could talk your ear off.

"Look, Enoch!" Carmen pointed to Ed. He was a couple of benches away, a notebook open on his lap.

"How you doing, Ed?" Carmen called out.

Ed smiled and waved us to join him. He wasn't as far gone as he was this morning, but he looked terrible.

"You write?" Carmen pointed to the journal jammed with small script.

"No, but I like stories. Hey, you guys know the story of the old man who was murdered on account of he had this evil eye?"

This story was more gruesome than the black cat one. The old man's body was cut up in pieces and put under the floorboards. The killer's guilty conscience gave him away. Ed could sure tell a scary story. Carmen said she wasn't sure it was a story.

"This guy's *loco,* Enoch. Be careful."

After dropping Carmen home, I saw Miguel chumming around with Dougie and his crew.

Chapter 15

Beware of funny feelings. All last week I had this
funny feeling that Adrian and Sam were planning a beat-down. I was right. I was taking a
shortcut through Poe Park when I saw them and
a couple of kids they recruited coming after me.
As luck would have it, a group of summer-campers
was getting off a yellow bus and heading into the
dead writer's cottage. Even though I wasn't wearing a T-shirt that said CAMP SUNSHINE, I joined the
end of their line. Nobody said anything. As the
curator took us on a tour of the house, I pre-
tended to hang on his every word. You don't say.
Wow. You know, I had been here before on a field
trip. All I remember about the writer who lived in

this cottage was that his young wife died there and shortly after that he was found dead of some unknown cause. Yeah, and he wrote this crazy weird poem we read last year about this black bird that keeps popping up and saying, "Nevermore." Spence and I made a joke of it. We even wrote HOMEWORK NEVERMORE in the boys' bathroom stall. But now all I was thinking about was the kids waiting for me outside. There was no way I'd get out of here without some serious injury. I tried real quick to remember some cool martial arts moves—you know, the kind you see in movies when the hero lets loose against a whole village.

Upstairs, we all crammed into a narrow room. It was the dying young wife's bedroom. If you asked me, it had a sad feel.

The next room was the video viewing room. While the curator fiddled with the VCR, I turned to go. I gave the little bedroom a sweeping glance. Hmm. Wooden floorboards like in Ed's story. Pull them up and you'd probably find some old guy's skull with an eyeball still in it. Creepy. I tiptoed down the creaky stairs.

In the foyer was a bulletin board with pictures

of visitors to the cottage. In the top left-hand corner was a Polaroid of Ed. It had to be him. He was way younger and looked like a regular person— nice clothes, clean-cut, and short hair. In the photo he's got his arms crisscrossed around this very pretty lady with a long red braid. She's about a head shorter than Ed, so he has to stoop over to put his face next to hers. Something funny must have happened because they're both laughing. Wonder what it was. I wanted to look at the photo some more, but I heard the curator directing the group down the stairs.

I unbolted the door and stepped out of the dark, gloomy cottage into the bright sun. Then bam. Right in my face, a fist crashed against my nose. I fell back, holding on to a wooden sign. Kids surrounded me. I only recognized Adrian and Sam. Just as I started to swing, everybody ran in all directions. I dropped to my knees. I knew it wasn't me who scared them off. Next thing I know, Miguel, Dougie, and his crew are picking me up. "Hey, are you all right?" Miguel held my chin and looked at my face. My nose hurt bad and my left eye was starting to close. "Nothing broken.

Come on, I'll take you to the salon." As we left, with my one good eye I could see the wooden sign I had fallen on. EDGAR ALLAN POE'S COTTAGE.

Mami had a fit when she saw me. "*Ay, Dios mío!* What happened?"

Miguel was only too happy to supply the info. He said a bunch of kids jumped me in Poe Park. *Por suerte,* luckily, he and his crew were there. Those kids weren't likely to try something like that anytime soon.

"Crew? Miguel."

"Just guys I hang with, Ma."

"You mean the gang you hang with," Julio said, handing me a towel with ice.

Miguel's comeback was rapid-fire fast: "Mind your business, gay boy."

"At least I know who I am." Skinny Julio was up in Miguel's face.

"Stop," Mami said. "*Por favor,* Miguel." She took his arm, but he yanked it away and stormed out of the salon.

I looked in the mirror, and the face that looked back at me was messed up, yet kind of cool, like a prizefighter's.

"Keep the ice on, Enoch," Mami snapped.

"What do you think I gave it to you for?" Julio echoed.

Figures. I get jumped and everybody is mad at me.

Later, much later, like two o'clock in the morning, I hear Mami cleaning out the refrigerator and singing Spanish songs. Whenever she does that, you know something is bugging her. Miguel isn't home. A while ago I went to get a glass of water. I stood there awhile, slowly drinking the water, thinking how I should say what was on my mind without it coming out wrong or stupid. Finally I said, "Listen, Ma, what do you think Miguel has been up to all this time? If you don't do something, he'll get in big trouble." Mami kept wiping the inside of the refrigerator. Without looking at me, she said that someday when I grew older, I'd understand. When I grow older—ha. That's so lame. I'll never tell my kids that. If I ever do, zap me to zero.

Chapter 16

It's 5 A.M. Someone's banging on our door. It's Julio. "Lourdes, Miguel has been picked up by the police along with some members of Firearms."

"*Que!*"

I got into the living room as Mami was calling Miriam at the precinct. By the expression on her face, I knew that what Julio had said was true. What happened? I followed Mami around the bedroom as she threw on a pair of jeans and a shirt. She kept saying how this was all her fault. What's your fault, Ma? What happened? Julio was behind us. "Don't worry. It must be some kind of mistake. You'll see. He was at the wrong place at the wrong time. I heard about this guy who—"

I was ready to scream, "Don't tell me about some guy. What happened to my brother?"

Mami reached over and gave me a hug. "*Hijo*, we'll call you when we get more information."

That was it. Mami and Julio were out the door before I had a chance to ask if I could come, too.

Six o'clock, seven o'clock—waiting for the phone to ring.

Eight o'clock. I'm looking through Miguel's stuff. You know, he collects comic books. He has a whole stack of them in his luggage. He must have brought them from Puerto Rico. Some are in Spanish, and others are in English. All of them are in plastic covers, mint condition. It also looked like Miguel saved every letter and card Mom sent him through the years, tied in a bundle with a sneaker lace. I'd like to read some of them, but I don't.

At around nine-thirty Carmen came over. She said I looked awful. No kidding. Would I like some breakfast? She pulled out a box of cereal and a carton of milk from her knapsack. "Don't look at me like that, Enoch. I bought this at the super-market. Want to see the receipt?"

While we ate, Carmen told me that Miriam called her from the precinct. Miguel is part of a lineup. Last night some kids near Fordham Road were mugged. Their gold chains were stolen and stuff. They claimed Firearms did it.

I told Carmen I didn't think Miguel would hurt anybody. Carmen kind of arched her eyebrows as if to say, Let's hope not, Enoch. I really hate this waiting around.

At eleven o'clock Carmen and I walked over to the precinct.

"What's the matter with you?" Julio shouted across the room when he spotted us. "Are you crazy?"

Mom jumped in. "Didn't I tell you to stay home? We have enough trouble here."

"Carmen, you know better." Miriam shook her head. We were just about to be sent away, when an officer walked by us, leading a beanpole-thin kid with a bandage on his head into a small room. He closed the door behind them.

"That's the last one," Miriam whispered.

So far nobody had identified Miguel. There was just this kid left. I wondered how Miguel felt, standing there waiting to be fingered. I knew my brother was capable of a lot of things. Could he draw blood just for some stupid chains? I wanted to believe in Miguel, but I couldn't. Spencer was the last person I believed in.

The police let Miguel go. Although the kids swore it was Firearms, it was dark and they couldn't make out their assailants.

We walked home from the precinct without saying a word.

Thank goodness, Julio can't hold his tongue for long.

"Miriam, I don't know how you do it, working near criminals day after day. There was one giving me the eye. Yes, he was. The one in the red shirt handcuffed to the chair. Looking at me like I was some common person, some *cualquiera.* Imagine that. He was kind of cute, though."

Everyone laughed, except Miguel. His head was lowered, his shoulders hunched.

When we got home, Mami sent me to my bedroom so she and Miguel could talk. Normally, I'm not a busybody, but I know when important stuff is going on, so I pressed my ear against the door. I heard Mami's voice.

"I've been thinking that you should go back to Puerto Rico. I can't be responsible for you. One of these days I'll get a call to come identify your body at the morgue. *Dios mío,* I couldn't take that."

"Ma, that's not going to happen. You think I jumped those kids. I didn't. I don't rob or do drugs."

"How do you expect me to believe that? You were sent here because your grandmother found drugs and cash hidden in your closet."

"It wasn't mine. I was holding it for somebody."

"Stop lying!" Mami raised her voice. "What next? Tell me. You hang out at all hours of the night with that Firearms. Even a child can see what is going on here. Miguel, I love you with all my heart. I am so sorry for not being there for you. But I just can't let this go on anymore. I've been feeling so guilty about the past that I haven't been strong enough to help you in the present.

Either clean up your act or you go back to P.R. Is that clear?"

"Hey, I'm not a little kid like Enoch. I don't need you. I never did. Never will!" Miguel slammed the bathroom door shut.

I thought about going out and offering some moral support, but I'd probably wind up getting caught in the cross fire, so I played with Isadore instead.

Before you know it, I fell asleep. Spencer came to me in a dream. In my dream, I wake up and Spencer is at the foot of my bed. He is wearing jeans and no shirt. He smiles at me, a goofy smile I remember so well. He doesn't say anything, just stands there smiling. I kneel up in bed, face-to-face with my dead friend. You weren't real with me, Spence. Get out of my dream. I want to forget I ever knew you. Let me forget. Please, buddy. Tears fill Spencer's eyes. Enormous tears fall along his cheeks down to his chest. Between his ribs, just above his belly button, I see a bullet hole.

"It doesn't have to end like this, Eno. You can make a difference."

Then I woke up for real. Miguel wasn't in his cot. He was sitting by the window. I could hear him sobbing.

Next day Ed didn't show up at the soup kitchen. Some other guy was doing his job. During game time I sat on an exercise mat, thinking: Make a difference. Yeah, right. I'm no action hero. No special powers here. Adrian and Sam were deep into a basketball game. At one point the ball rolled my way. I threw it back. Sam made a cool dunk. He looked around, grinning ear to ear. Our eyes met for a sec. I grinned, giving Sam the thumbs-up. He nodded, then looked away. Man, I didn't need enemies. I told as much to Willy, who agreed. Then for no reason at all, I told Willy about all the problems we were having at home with Miguel. Willy listened. Then for no reason at all, Willy told me that he'd always wished he had a brother. Sometimes he gets lonely being the only child. I told Willy he could come stay over at my house anytime he wanted. He could have Miguel, too. Just kidding.

Carmen walked by, and I asked her if she had anything to eat. *Nada.* Zip. Her knapsack was empty, for a change. Good news, huh? But not for my stomach. It was mad grumbling.

As soon as camp let out, I went to buy a super-duper slice of pizza with extra everything. Afterward, I rode my bike around Poe Park. That's when I noticed Ed. What if Ed was short for Edgar, like the dead writer who lived in the cottage? Spooky. Who knows? All I know is that Ed was drunk. People must have thought I was crazy for sitting next to him. I started chitchatting like everything was fine. "Hey, Ed. I missed you at the soup kitchen. They got this other guy, but he's not so good. He's kind of sloppy." Ed nodded, listening. I kept talking. "You know, you shouldn't drink so much. It's bad for you. Makes you sick. Did something awful happen to you to make you this way?"

Ed looked toward the Concourse, his face twisted. "Years ago my wife died. I haven't been the same since."

I said I was sorry. Then I asked Ed if that was his wife in the picture tacked on the bulletin board at Poe Cottage. For a while Ed didn't say a word. I thought maybe he was mad at me for bringing up the subject. Then Ed cleared his throat.

"Annie and I visited the cottage for her birthday."

Ed said that he met Annie in the Peace Corps. They taught at a school they helped build in Guatemala. He talked about when he lifted Annie onto his shoulders so she could whitewash the ceiling. She dripped paint all over his head. Another time, when he got so sick from drinking the water that he thought he was going to die, Annie was there all night, reading him selections from their favorite author, the one who lived in Poe Cottage. Life was wonderful. Ed and Annie married. Ed even landed a dream job as an adjunct college English professor. They were so happy.

Then Annie died.

Ed said that losing her was all his fault. They had the worst argument ever. Annie told him she was expecting a child. Ed blew. He wasn't ready for a baby. Work responsibilities at the university were piling up and up. Money was tight. He started saying a lot of things he didn't mean. He sounded just like his old man. It was their first fight. The next morning Annie left to visit a friend in Baltimore. Ed never saw her again. The commuter plane she was on crashed.

"I ruined everything, Enoch. I had a perfect life, but I didn't know it."

Boy. What do you say to that? I just sat there. Then I asked Ed something so right-in-front-of-your-nose that it was idiotic. I asked Ed if he loved Annie. I wanted him to say it. I don't know why.

"Yes, I loved her very much. Annie was my life."

I told Ed that I wished people we loved didn't have to die.

Ed leaned back on the bench. He told me about this group of people who shut themselves in this palace to get away from a death plague. They had a masquerade ball, only this strange visitor shows up and he's really the plague in a person's body. Then the next thing you know, he finishes off everybody at the party. So the moral of the story is you can't escape death so make sure you check IDs at the door. Ha. It was a creepy story, the kind Ed is so good at telling. I asked Ed what the plague was, but he didn't answer. He had fallen asleep on the bench.

I'd like to help Ed out. He's good people. Just kind of messed up in the head. Can you blame him?

Chapter 17

Everybody is going nuts. Miguel moved out. He took his things and he's on the street somewhere. Mami and Miriam are looking for him while Julio tends to the customers. Carmen's here giving shampoos and not doing a bad job of it. Julio throws me a broom.

"Don't just stand there. Sweep."

Hours go by. We close up the salon. No sign of Miguel. All night Mami keeps pacing the apartment, saying that she shouldn't have given him an ultimatum.

The *viejas* are in the living room. I don't know who called them, but they're here with their rosaries and candles. Even though I close my bedroom door, I still hear them praying. *Dios te salve Maria, llena eres de gracia* . . . I wish Mami would ask them to leave. Miguel isn't dead. Nah. That's not going to happen. Not if I can help it. I am going to find my brother and bring him home. In a little while, when Mami's asleep, I'll scoot down the fire escape. Right now I've got to tune out the *viejas. Dios te salve Maria, llena eres de gracia* . . . Over and over and over.

What! It's morning. I am so mad at myself. I can't believe I nodded off. I should have been out there looking for Miguel. Maybe I would have found him and he'd be home by now, sleeping on his cot, nice and safe. But no, I'm taking zzzs like I haven't a care in the world. Weak, Enoch, weak. I'd diss myself proper, but there's no time to lose.

Plan. I'll pretend like I'm going to camp, but I'll be checking the streets, asking around, doing like they do in movies when they're looking for a missing person. I'll need a picture of Miguel and some money, just in case I've got to slip somebody a five to jog their memory.

Mami's curled up on the sofa, clutching the phone. She hears me walking around and wakes up all startled.

"Miguel?"

"No, Ma. Go back to sleep."

I'd fix her some breakfast, only I'm so anxious to get going.

This was me two weeks ago, running out of my building with one thought in my mind. Find Miguel. I already knew where to start looking.

Only Carmen was sitting on the stoop. She said she wasn't sure whether I was going to camp with Miguel missing and all. I told her to go without me. I had things to do. She said that she wanted to help. That was that. The girl put herself smack in my way. She said I had been there for her; now it was her turn to be there for me. What could I say? Maybe with the two of us looking we'd find Miguel faster.

I told Carmen that our first stop was Spencer's building. I'd been avoiding going there all summer. I knew the place would be full of Spence, and it was.

"What's the matter?" Carmen squeezed my hand. We took the elevator to Spencer's floor. I knocked on Spencer's door. It opened a crack. Spencer's little brother Leon recognized me quick.

"Hey, Grandma, it's Enoch and a friend."

The little kid flashed a great big goofy smile. Mrs. Bandy called from inside, "Well, let them in." There were boxes all over the apartment. Mrs. Bandy sat at the kitchen table, busily wrapping some glass figurines in newspaper. "Excuse the mess. Eno, sugar, come here and give me a kiss. We certainly have missed you around here."

"You're really moving?" I asked, looking around.

Mrs. Bandy nodded. "It will be a new start. Sit down. Hello, Carmen, sweetie. Leon, bring them some orange juice with ice. Enoch, I am glad you paid us a call. Spencer thought a great deal of you."

I wished she hadn't said that. It made me sad—sad on top of sad, layers of sad. I wondered if Mrs. Bandy knew about Spencer's drug running. I wasn't going to tell her if she didn't. Instead, I asked her if Dougie was around.

"Hasn't anyone told you? Dougie's not living here anymore. I don't even know where he's staying. He left about the same time Spencer passed." Mrs. Bandy's eyes looked into mine. "Are you in any trouble?"

"No, my brother is. I'm afraid for him."

"Oh my, oh my." Mrs. Bandy put her face close to mine. "You are shouldering a lot, little one."

Though Mrs. Bandy was talking directly to me, she looked to the side and I knew she was thinking aloud.

"Nowadays it seems that kids can't be kids anymore. Bad all around tempting them, making them do things that they have better sense than to do. We adults don't realize what's going on until it is too late. I failed my grandbaby. I should have been aware. Enoch, you haven't tasted your juice. . . ."

When Carmen and I got up to leave, Mrs. Bandy said that she had something to give me. Something that she knew Spencer would have liked me to have. She went into her room to get it but returned after a few minutes, all flustered.

134

"Enoch, I can't find it. With this move, things don't stay in one place long. When I find it, I'll send it on to you."

I stood at the front door, knowing that the next thing I should do was say good-bye. Carmen was waiting for me in the hallway. I threw Leon a play punch.

"Well, I hope everything works out all right for your brother." Mrs. Bandy smiled sadly. "Be careful, sugar."

"The elevator's here," Carmen called.

I gave Mrs. Bandy a kiss on the cheek. "Spencer was good! Good." I blurted it out.

"Yes, he was." Mrs. Bandy hugged me hard.

It's incredible the ground Carmen and I covered— we took the subway to 161st Street near Yankee Stadium and then walked straight up the Grand Concourse past Fordham Road to somewhere near Woodlawn Cemetery. Along the way we looked in the handball courts. Everywhere there was a pack of kids hanging out, we'd think, Miguel has got to be here, but no such luck.

It was getting dark. Carmen looked real tired, but she didn't complain. The soles of my feet were hurting. All this walking for nothing. We hadn't come close to finding Miguel. Looking through the gate at all those tombstones, I wondered if it was some kind of bad omen that we ended up by a cemetery.

"Let's go home," I said.

"Yeah, Enoch." Carmen sounded relieved.

Back in the neighborhood, at the sight of the hot-dog vendor in front of Poe Park, my stomach went wild. We hadn't eaten all day. Carmen and I bought two hot dogs apiece loaded with onions.

The food really perked us up. We started talking about other places we could look for Miguel. Carmen said it was too bad we couldn't try the crack houses around here. Maybe that's where Firearms was holed up. When I said, "Hey, why can't we check them out? That's not a bad idea," Carmen shot me a look like I suddenly had a hot-dog–shaped nose or something.

"Forget it, Enoch."

"I wouldn't go inside. Just stake it out, like in the movies, you know?"

"Then what would you do?"

"Whatever I have to."

"*Estúpido*," Carmen practically spit the word out. "*Estúpido.*"

I couldn't argue with that. I was stupid all right—me up against a crack house. What was I thinking? I hated the thought of Miguel being in one of those places. Man, any way you shook it, this world looked lousy. I scanned Poe Park. There was Ed on a bench, teetering over, drinking from a bottle—kids playing and people talking around him like he didn't exist.

Spencer's voice was in my ear. "Eno, it doesn't have to be like this." Yeah, whatever you say, buddy.

Sitting on the steps of the rotunda was Fire-arms. Miguel was wearing a red bandanna. He had this *malo* gangster face.

Carmen was talking nonstop about what her mother told her goes on in crack houses.

I walked to the rotunda.

Miguel's eyes caught me coming and then looked away. I made my way through the Fire-arms crew. I heard Dougie: "Hey, Eno." I went for Miguel. Grabbing his biceps, I said, "Let's talk."

"I've got nothing to say to you."

I saw the shiny gold necklace that hung around his neck.

"I thought you told Mami—"

"You don't understand. Go."

"But Miguel, come on—"

"Leave me alone."

"Miguel."

"Are you deaf? I don't want you around here. Forget me." Miguel pushed me away.

I felt like a baby pulling a tantrum. "It's okay, Miguel. Let's go home. We'll work things out. Please. Let's go. It's not too late. Please."

Everyone was looking now.

"Calm down, little man." Hands took my shoulders and spun me around. It was Dougie. "This is where your brother belongs now. It'll be okay. We'll take care of him. Don't worry. Now, go on. We've got important business to discuss." Dougie turned his attention to Firearms.

Right then I should have walked. It would have been the smart thing to do. Carmen's eyes were begging me to do just that. She was standing a few feet away, watching.

I took a breath and said, "Yeah, Dougie, you'll take care of Miguel like you took care of Spencer."

"What?"

"It's your fault Spencer's dead."

Dougie's face went hard. "That wasn't my doing. It was someone messing with a gun."

"You know what I mean. You were his cousin. He looked up to you. You were supposed to show him right from wrong. You had the responsibility. Punk!" I stuck my finger in Dougie's face and yelled to the rooftops loud, "Punk! Kid killer! Punk!"

"Shut up!" Dougie lunged at me and with his two hands pulled me forward by my shirt collar, twisting it tighter and tighter, choking me. "Shut up! I told you Spencer's death wasn't my doing."

I heard Carmen crying, whimpering. People gathered around.

Suddenly Miguel was between Dougie and me. He put his hands over Dougie's hands. "Easy, he didn't mean anything. Right, Enoch?" Dougie's eyes were red. "Your brother should watch his mouth. Spence was my heart. I thought I was doing right by showing him the ropes. It's not like

I pulled the trigger. It wasn't my fault. How can people say that?"

"I know. I know," Miguel whispered as he loosened Dougie's grip until I was free. I sat on the rotunda steps, gasping for air as Firearms, along with Miguel, walked out of Poe Park.

It wasn't fair. First I lost Spencer and now Miguel. Carmen was at my side. "Are you okay, Enoch? I was scared."

When I got home, Mami looked at my face and without asking questions she hugged me. I burrowed myself into her. Later, while we ate dinner, I mentioned that I had seen Miguel hanging with Firearms, but I didn't say anything about Dougie. Mami asked how Miguel looked. Okay, Ma. Did you speak to him, Enoch? Not really, Ma.

Chapter 18

During the next couple of days, I'd see Miguel around the neighborhood. I'd spot him or he'd spot me. We'd look at each other, but we wouldn't step forward to even say hello. It was so strange.

Once I was with Willy and we were talking to Ed, when Miguel sent word with one of his crew that little kids shouldn't be talking to drunks. I sent word back, asking, "Miguel, when are you coming home?"

At night I'd lie in bed, thinking about my brother. How was he doing? Where was he staying? I kept looking at his folded-up cot, wishing he was there. I didn't care if he hogged up the bathroom or lifted weights in the center of the room. I kind of liked the way he called me *hermanito*. The way he taught me wrestling moves. Didn't we make a good team pedaling that boat in the Bear Mountain pond? Why didn't I tell him that I was getting used to having him around? Maybe I could have kept him from doing bad things. Before sleeping, I would close my eyes and ask Spence to do the *angel de la guarda* thing and watch over Miguel.

Then the other night, about three weeks after Miguel moved out, I heard someone in the room. It was Miguel. In the moonlight, I could see his shadow looking for something inside the cot. I sat up in bed.

"Miguel, you came back."

Miguel jumped up, startled. *"Hermanito."*

I told Miguel how happy I was to see him and how Mami had been a wreck since he left. Miguel sat on the corner of the bed, listening. He had one hand under the front of his T-shirt. I got up to turn on the lights.

"No, leave them off." Miguel reached out and

touched my arm, but I'd already switched them on. I saw Miguel's face, bruised, and his knuckles, cut and bloody.

"You're hurt. What happened?"

"This is nothing. *Nada.* You should see the other guy." Miguel's laugh sounded empty, strange.

"I'll wake Ma."

Miguel said he didn't want to bother her; besides, he wasn't staying. I noticed Miguel was still holding something under his shirt, and I knew what it was. Miguel started telling me about this guy in Firearms who challenged him. The fight was all about respect and survival. "Enoch, you can't let people disrespect you. Can't let that pass. Remember the other day, you almost crossed the line with Dougie. You're lucky I was there. You realize you could have ended up like your friend Spencer. In this world you have to think quick, act crazy, and be prepared to follow through. Even if it means—" Miguel motioned to what he was holding under his shirt.

"Miguel. You don't have to go it alone. We're family."

Miguel shook his head.

"Nah, you don't get it." Miguel's voice was rising. "No one has been there for me, ever."

"Miguel, give us a chance."

"Man, why should I?"

" 'Cause I need you. I didn't think I did, but I do. I need you, *hermano*."

Miguel got up.

"If you leave, who's going to show me how to wrestle, lift weights. Or kiss girls. What about"—now I was stalling—"Isadore's condo with the heating unit?"

"Stop, Enoch, stop. I'm sorry." My brother was leaving.

"Don't go. *Por favor.*"

"I can't stay. Not for you and not for Mami."

I was blubbering. "Go, bro punk. You're just like Dougie. He let Spencer down. You're letting me down."

Miguel groaned. "*Hermanito,* don't lay this on me."

"Go with that gun you're carrying under your shirt. Put my face on whoever you shoot."

"You stupid, stupid kid." Miguel whipped the

.38 out and waved it in the air. He turned and kicked the dresser again and again, banging the drawers. "I ought to blow my brains out," he cried.

I jumped on Miguel's back, wrapping my arms and legs around him. I had to get the gun, to take it away from him before—

"Get off! I don't want to hurt you!" Miguel yelled as he slammed me against the dresser, but I wouldn't let go. The .38 touched where my hands clung to Miguel's chest. The barrel was pointed up. I looked into it, looking for Spencer—buddy, help me!

I don't know how I did it, but somehow I managed to smack the gun out of Miguel's hand. It flew across the floor. Next thing I knew, I followed, crashing against the closet door. Miguel was crying. Mami was in the room. When she took hold of Miguel, he fought like an animal to get out of her embrace. I jumped in, grabbing them close. We rolled onto the bed. Miguel's loud sobs filled the room. He wasn't struggling anymore. The .38 lay on the floor next to the window. Mami was stroking Miguel's hair, humming a tune she used to hum to me when I was little. I closed my eyes and leaned my head on my brother's shoulder. I knew that if I looked up, there'd be Spence standing at the foot of the bed, seeing us through this night.

Chapter 19

Miguel stayed. That's all I'll say about that, because you never know. Sometimes I think the word *forever* is so fake. *Boom.* Bad things happen to you—now deal. That's been my summer. Right now we are topping it off with a little celebration, a Labor Day bash at the salon. It was Carmen's idea. Mami said, "Sure. *Cómo no!*" She's happy these days.

The music and the food is *caliente*—hot, hot, hot. I have so many "You know what?"s to tell. Like, you know what? I found out yesterday that Willy is going to be my classmate at the new charter school. Willy's a funny guy. He says that in a couple of months we'll be running the place. I believe it.

You know what else? Ed dropped by. I invited him, thinking he'd never come. Here I am, sucking on my fourth ice pop, and in walks Ed. He washed his hair and even put on a semi-clean shirt. In a sec, Carmen, Willy, and I were around him. Everybody else kind of just froze and stared at him. Miguel was ready to tell him to beat it, but Mami intercepted: "A friend of Enoch's is a friend of mine. Let me fix you a plate of food." Whew.

What else? Mrs. Bandy came by with Kareem, Leon, and Baby Omarr. Next week the movers will take them away from our neighborhood. I think I'll always think of my buddy Spence whenever I pass that apartment building. "Enoch, I found it." Mrs. Bandy pulled a manila envelope out of her bag. "Sugar, I know Spencer would like you to have this."

I took it and put it away for later.

All in all, it was a cool *fiesta*.

As we were winding down, Dougie and his crew passed by the salon a couple of times. Mrs. Bandy hadn't left; Baby Omarr was asleep in her arms. Dougie kept glancing her way. I could tell that he really wanted to come in, but he couldn't break with his crew. I caught Miguel looking at Dougie. Remember what I said about forever. Mami wants Miguel and Julio to attend night school and get their GEDs. Julio and Miguel in the same class. *Ay!*

The last "You know what?" is that I brought Isadore to the party. I wanted him there. Most of the party, with the exception of when I was dancing, I held Izzy. So I was holding him when everybody left. I opened the envelope Mrs. Bandy gave me.

Inside was a picture Spencer drew of us together. In the picture we're like superheroes, with muscles bulging out all over the place. Spencer wrote at the bottom, *Enoch and Spencer, Friends to the End.*

I lost my best friend this summer. There are days I'm doing okay, then something happens and I'm right back in that sad place, missing Spencer. Like now. In my mind I see Spence and me in so many good-time scenes.

I feel Isadore climbing up to my shoulder,

nudging my chin with his head. It's like he wants me to tell Spencer something, since he can't. The words are stuck in his iguana throat. Stuck in mine, too.

Maybe it's, "Peace, buddy. Good-bye."